LITERARY TOUCHSTONE CLASSICS™
P.O. Box 658 Clayton, Delaware 19938 • www.prestwickhouse.com

Senior Editor: Paul Moliken

Editor: Lisa M. Miller and Stacey MacPherson

Reviewing Teacher: Barbara Bretherick, Wellington, FL

Cover Design: Kyle Price

Production: Dana Kerr

P.O. Box 658 • Clayton, Delaware 19938

Tel: 1.800.932.4593

Fax: 1.888.718.9333

Web: www.prestwickhouse.com

Prestwick House Teaching Units™, Activity Packs™, and Response Journals™ are the perfect complement for these editions. To purchase teaching resources for this book, visit www.prestwickhouse.com

This Prestwick House edition is an unabridged republication, with minor emendations, of thirteen of O. Henry's short stories, taken from various sources in the public domain.

ISBN-10 1-58049-347-5
ISBN-13 978-1-58049-347-5

THE BEST OF O. HENRY:

The Gift of the Magi and *Twelve Other Stories*

CONTENTS

Notes

What is a literary classic and why are these classic works important to the world?

A literary classic is a work of the highest excellence that has something important to say about life and/or the human condition and says it with great artistry. A classic, through its enduring presence, has withstood the test of time and is not bound by time, place, or customs. It speaks to us today as forcefully as it spoke to people one hundred or more years ago, and as forcefully as it will speak to people of future generations. For this reason, a classic is said to have universality.

O. Henry

O. Henry is the pen name of William Sydney Porter, who was born in Greensboro, NC, on September 11, 1862. He did not receive a formal education and, at twenty years of age, moved to Texas, where he worked on a sheep ranch.

In 1887, he married Athol Estes Roach, supposedly the model for Della in "The Gift of the Magi," O. Henry's most popular story. They had two children, a son (who died a few hours after birth) and a daughter. A year later, he obtained a job at a bank, but was accused of embezzlement and served time in Ohio Penitentiary. However, it was this imprisonment that led directly to O. Henry's career as a writer; in 1902, after three years in prison, he settled in New York with his new name and nearly a dozen short stories ready to be published.

For three years, O. Henry wrote short stories every week for the *World*, a New York newspaper. *Cabbages and Kings*, his first collection of short stories, was published in 1904. These stories became extremely popular throughout the United States, and O. Henry's next book, *The Four Million*, cemented his reputation as a vivid portrayer of life in New York City.

However, his personal life was destroyed by a failed marriage, bad financial dealings, and heavy drinking. O. Henry died of complications due to alcoholism, penniless, on June 5, 1910.

The derivation of his pseudonym is unclear: It may be related to a family cat, the name of the prison warden, or a name in a book he read in jail.

Reading Pointers

Reading Pointers for Sharper Insights

As you read this collection of the best of O. Henry's short stories, keep the following points in mind:

Surprise Endings

- The endings, while unexpected, always seem appropriate to the characters.
- The surprise ending usually shows O. Henry's philosophy about America: Wrongs are made right, the villains are punished, and the good are rewarded.
- Hints that point toward the climax are inevitably provided throughout the story.
- The use of coincidences in the stories helps make the endings more plausible, but may also make the plot seem overly manipulated, just to achieve the surprise.

The Depiction of Poverty and Wealth

- Having no money is not indicative of being poor.
- There is a kind of nobility, even in the most poverty-stricken lives.
- For a few, one tragedy will lead to another.
- O. Henry usually portrays poverty sympathetically and condemns the forces that cause it.
- Money is no barrier when it comes to love.

Settings

- New York City and its surroundings near the beginning of the 20th century
- Texas, or the West, at the turn of the century

Characters

- ordinary people in menial jobs struggling to survive
- con men who derive their income from swindling innocent victims
- people, both rich and poor, caught up by circumstances beyond their control

- O. Henry's sympathetic portrayal of his characters
- immigrants or first-generation Americans
- the underdog
- self-sacrificing heroes

Style

- dialects and slang
- digressions and asides to the reader
- the use of simile, metaphor, personification, and allusion
- puns, malapropisms, and excessive vocabulary used for humor
- lightheartedness and sensitivity

Love

- If love is even slightly dishonest, it will fail.
- Love is available to everyone.
- True love is more valuable than money and will conquer nearly any evil.
- Love is frequently unexpected.

The Furnished Room

RESTLESS, SHIFTING, FUGACIOUS as time itself is a certain vast bulk of the population of the red brick district of the lower West Side.† Homeless, they have a hundred homes. They flit from furnished room to furnished room, transients forever—transients in abode, transients in heart and mind. They sing "Home, Sweet Home"† in ragtime;† they carry their *lares et penates*† in a bandbox; their vine is entwined about a picture hat;† a rubber plant is their fig tree.

Hence the houses of this district, having had a thousand dwellers, should have a thousand tales to tell, mostly dull ones, no doubt; but it would be strange if there could not be found a ghost or two in the wake of all these vagrant guests.

One evening after dark a young man prowled among these crumbling red mansions, ringing their bells. At the twelfth he rested his lean hand-baggage upon the step and wiped the dust from his hatband and forehead. The bell sounded faint and far away in some remote, hollow depths.

To the door of this, the twelfth house whose bell he had rung, came a housekeeper who made him think of an unwholesome, surfeited worm† that had eaten its nut to a hollow shell and now sought to fill the vacancy with edible lodgers.

He asked if there was a room to let.

"Come in," said the housekeeper. Her voice came from her throat; her

†Terms marked in the text with (†) can be looked up in the Glossary for additional information.

throat seemed lined with fur. "I have the third-floor back, vacant since a week back. Should you wish to look at it?"

The young man followed her up the stairs. A faint light from no particular source mitigated the shadows of the halls. They trod noiselessly upon a stair carpet that its own loom would have forsworn.† It seemed to have become vegetable; to have degenerated in that rank, sunless air to lush lichen or spreading moss that grew in patches to the staircase and was viscid under the foot like organic matter. At each turn of the stairs were vacant niches in the wall. Perhaps plants had once been set within them. If so they had died in that foul and tainted air. It may be that statues of the saints had stood there, but it was not difficult to conceive that imps and devils had dragged them forth in the darkness and down to the unholy depths of some furnished pit below.

"This is the room," said the housekeeper, from her furry throat. "It's a nice room. It ain't often vacant. I had some most elegant people in it last summer—no trouble at all, and paid in advance to the minute. The water's at the end of the hall. Sprowls and Mooney kept it three months. They done a vaudeville sketch. Miss B'retta Sprowls—you may have heard of her—Oh, that was just the stage names—right there over the dresser is where the marriage certificate hung, framed. The gas is here, and you see there is plenty of closet room. It's a room everybody likes. It never stays idle long."

"Do you have many theatrical people rooming here?" asked the young man.

"They comes and goes. A good proportion of my lodgers is connected with the theatres. Yes, sir, this is the theatrical district. Actor people never stays long anywhere. I get my share. Yes, they comes and they goes."

He engaged the room, paying for a week in advance. He was tired, he said, and would take possession at once. He counted out the money. The room had been made ready, she said, even to towels and water. As the housekeeper moved away he put, for the thousandth time, the question that he carried at the end of his tongue.

"A young girl—Miss Vashner—Miss Eloise Vashner—do you remember such a one among your lodgers? She would be singing on the stage, most likely. A fair girl, of medium height and slender, with reddish, gold hair and a dark mole near her left eyebrow."

"No, I don't remember the name. Them stage people has names they change as often as their rooms. They comes and they goes. No, I don't call that one to mind."

No. Always no. Five months of ceaseless interrogation and the inevitable negative. So much time spent by day in questioning managers, agents, schools and choruses; by night among the audiences of theatres from all-star casts down to music halls so low that he dreaded to find what he most hoped for. He who had loved her best had tried to find her. He was sure that since her disappearance from home this great, water-girt† city held her somewhere, but it was like a monstrous quicksand, shifting its particles constantly, with no foundation, its upper granules of to-day buried tomorrow in ooze and slime.

The furnished room received its latest guest with a first glow of pseudo-hospitality, a hectic, haggard, perfunctory welcome like the specious smile of a demirep.† The sophistical comfort came in reflected gleams from the decayed furniture, the ragged brocade upholstery of a couch and two chairs, a foot-wide cheap pier-glass between the two windows, from one or two gilt picture frames and a brass bedstead in a corner.

The guest reclined, inert, upon a chair, while the room, confused in speech as though it were an apartment in Babel,† tried to discourse to him of its divers tenantry.

A polychromatic rug like some brilliant-flowered rectangular, tropical islet lay surrounded by a billowy sea of soiled matting. Upon the gay-papered wall were those pictures that pursue the homeless one from house to house—The Huguenot† Lovers, The First Quarrel, The Wedding Breakfast, Psyche at the Fountain.† The mantel's chastely severe outline was ingloriously veiled behind some pert drapery drawn rakishly askew like the sashes of the Amazonian ballet. Upon it was some desolate flotsam cast aside by the room's marooned when a lucky sail had borne them to a fresh port—a trifling vase or two, pictures of actresses, a medicine bottle, some stray cards out of a deck.

One by one, as the characters of a cryptograph become explicit, the little signs left by the furnished room's procession of guests developed a significance. The threadbare space in the rug in front of the dresser told that lovely women had marched in the throng. Tiny fingerprints on the wall spoke of little prisoners trying to feel their way to sun and air. A splattered stain, raying like the shadow of a bursting bomb, witnessed where a hurled glass or bottle had splintered with its contents against the wall. Across the pier glass had been scrawled with a diamond in staggering letters the name "Marie." It seemed that the succession of dwellers in the furnished room had turned in fury—perhaps tempted beyond forbearance by its garish coldness—and wreaked upon it their passions. The furniture was chipped and bruised; the couch, distorted by bursting springs, seemed a horrible monster† that had been slain during the stress of some grotesque convulsion. Some more potent upheaval had cloven a great slice from the marble mantel. Each plank in the floor owned its particular cant and shriek as from a separate and individual agony. It seemed incredible that all this malice and injury had been wrought upon the room by those who had called it for a time their home; and yet it may have been the cheated home instinct surviving blindly, the resentful rage at false household gods that had kindled their wrath. A hut that is our own we can sweep and adorn and cherish.

The young tenant in the chair allowed these thoughts to file, soft-shod, through his mind, while there drifted into the room furnished sounds and furnished scents. He heard in one room a tittering and incontinent, slack laughter; in others the monologue of a scold, the rattling of dice, a lullaby, and one crying dully; above him a banjo tinkled with spirit. Doors banged somewhere; the elevated trains roared intermittently; a cat yowled miserably upon a back fence. And he breathed the breath of the house—a dank savour rather than a smell—a cold, musty effluvium as from underground vaults mingled with the reeking exhalations of linoleum and mildewed and rotten woodwork.

Then, suddenly, as he rested there, the room was filled with the strong, sweet odor of mignonette. It came as upon a single buffet of wind with such sureness and fragrance and emphasis that it almost seemed a living visitant. And the man cried aloud: "What, dear?" as if he had been called, and sprang up and faced about. The rich odor clung to him and wrapped him around. He reached out his arms for it, all his senses for the time confused and commingled. How could one be peremptorily called by an odor? Surely it must have been a sound. But, was it not the sound that had touched, that had caressed him?

"She has been in this room," he cried, and he sprang to wrest from it a token, for he knew he would recognize the smallest thing that had belonged to her or that she had touched. This enveloping scent of mignonette, the odor that she had loved and made her own—whence came it?

The room had been but carelessly set in order. Scattered upon the flimsy dresser scarf were half a dozen hairpins—those discreet, indistinguishable friends of womankind, feminine of gender, infinite of mood and uncommunicative of tense. These he ignored, conscious of their triumphant lack of identity. Ransacking the drawers of the dresser he came upon a discarded, tiny, ragged handkerchief. He pressed it to his face. It was racy and insolent with heliotrope; he hurled it to the floor. In another drawer he found odd buttons, a theatre programme, a pawnbroker's card, two lost marshmallows, a book on the divination of dreams. In the last was a woman's black satin hair bow, which halted him, poised between ice and fire. But the black satin hair bow also is femininity's demure, impersonal, common ornament, and tells no tales.

And then he traversed the room like a hound on the scent, skimming the walls, considering the corners of the bulging matting on his hands and knees, rummaging mantel and tables, the curtains and hangings, the drunken cabinet in the corner, for a visible sign, unable to perceive that she was there beside, around, against, within, above him, clinging to him, wooing him, calling him so poignantly through the finer senses that even his grosser ones became cognizant of the call. Once again he answered loudly: "Yes, dear!" and turned, wild-eyed, to gaze on vacancy, for he could not yet discern form and color and love and outstretched arms in the odor of mignonette. Oh, God! whence that odor, and since when have odors had a voice to call? Thus he groped.

He burrowed in crevices and corners, and found corks and cigarettes. These he passed in passive contempt. But once he found in a fold of the matting a half-smoked cigar, and this he ground beneath his heel with a green and trenchant oath. He sifted the room from end to end. He found dreary and ignoble small records of many a peripatetic tenant; but of her whom he sought, and who may have lodged there, and whose spirit seemed to hover there, he found no trace.

And then he thought of the housekeeper.

He ran from the haunted room downstairs and to a door that showed a crack of light. She came out to his knock. He smothered his excitement as best he could.

"Will you tell me, madam," he besought her, "who occupied the room I have before I came?"

"Yes, sir. I can tell you again. 'Twas Sprowls and Mooney, as I said. Miss B'retta Sprowls it was in the theatres, but Missis Mooney she was. My house is well known for respectability. The marriage certificate hung, framed, on a nail over—"

"What kind of a lady was Miss Sprowls—in looks, I mean?"

"Why, black-haired, sir, short, and stout, with a comical face. They left a week ago Tuesday."

"And before they occupied it?"

"Why, there was a single gentleman connected with the draying business. He left owing me a week. Before him was Missis Crowder and her two children, that stayed four months; and back of them was old Mr. Doyle, whose sons paid for him. He kept the room six months. That goes back a year, sir, and further I do not remember."

He thanked her and crept back to his room. The room was dead. The essence that had vivified it was gone. The perfume of mignonette had departed. In its place was the old, stale odor of moldy house furniture, of atmosphere in storage.

The ebbing of his hope drained his faith. He sat staring at the yellow, singing gaslight. Soon he walked to the bed and began to tear the sheets into strips. With the blade of his knife he drove them tightly into every crevice around windows and door. When all was snug and taut he turned out the light, turned the gas full on again and laid himself gratefully upon the bed.

* * * * * *

It was Mrs. McCool's night to go with the can for beer. So she fetched it and sat with Mrs. Purdy in one of those subterranean retreats where housekeepers foregather and the worm dieth seldom.

"I rented out my third-floor-back this evening," said Mrs. Purdy, across a fine circle of foam. "A young man took it. He went up to bed two hours ago."

"Now, did ye, Mrs. Purdy, ma'am?" said Mrs. McCool, with intense admiration. "You do be a wonder for rentin' rooms of that kind. And did ye tell him, then?" she concluded in a husky whisper, laden with mystery.

"Rooms," said Mrs. Purdy, in her furriest tones, "are furnished for to rent. I did not tell him, Mrs. McCool."

"'Tis right ye are, ma'am; 'tis by renting rooms we kape alive. Ye have the rale sense for business, ma'am. There be many people will rayjict† the rentin' of a room if they be tould a suicide has been after dyin' in the bed of it."

"As you say, we has our living to be making," remarked Mrs. Purdy.

"Yis, ma'am; 'tis true. 'Tis just one wake ago this day I helped ye lay out the third-floor-back. A pretty slip of a colleen† she was to be killin' herself wid the gas—a swate little face she had, Mrs. Purdy, ma'am."

"She'd a-been called handsome, as you say," said Mrs. Purdy, assenting but critical, "but for that mole she had a-growin' by her left eyebrow.† Do fill up your glass again, Mrs. McCool."

The Last Leaf

In a little district west of Washington Square the streets have run crazy and broken themselves into small strips called "places." These "places" make strange angles and curves. One street crosses itself a time or two. An artist once discovered a valuable possibility in this street. Suppose a collector with a bill for paints, paper and canvas should, in traversing this route, suddenly meet himself coming back, without a cent having been paid on account!

So, to quaint old Greenwich Village† the art people soon came prowling, hunting for north windows and eighteenth-century gables and Dutch attics and low rents. Then they imported some pewter mugs and a chafing dish or two from Sixth avenue, and became a "colony."

At the top of a squatty, three-story brick Sue and Johnsy had their studio. "Johnsy" was familiar for Joanna. One was from Maine; the other from California. They had met at the *table d'hote*† of an Eighth street "Delmonico's,"† and found their tastes in art, chicory salad and bishop sleeves† so congenial that the joint studio resulted.

That was in May. In November a cold, unseen stranger, whom the doctors called Pneumonia, stalked about the colony, touching one here and there with his icy fingers. Over on the east side this ravager strode boldly, smiting his victims by scores, but his feet trod slowly through the maze of the narrow and moss-grown "places."

Mr. Pneumonia† was not what you would call a chivalric old gentleman. A mite of a little woman with blood thinned by California zephyrs was hardly fair game for the red-fisted, short-breathed old duffer. But Johnsy he smote; and she lay, scarcely moving, on her painted iron bedstead, looking through the small Dutch window-panes at the blank side of the next brick house.

One morning the busy doctor invited Sue into the hallway with a shaggy, gray eyebrow.

"She has one chance in—let us say, ten," he said, as he shook down the mercury in his clinical thermometer. "And that chance is for her to want to live. This way people have of lining-up on the side of the undertaker makes the entire pharmacopeia look silly. Your little lady has made up her mind that she's not going to get well. Has she anything on her mind?"

"She—she wanted to paint the Bay of Naples† some day," said Sue.

"Paint?—bosh! Has she anything on her mind worth thinking about twice—a man, for instance?"

"A man?" said Sue, with a jew's-harp† twang in her voice. "Is a man worth—but, no, doctor; there is nothing of the kind."

"Well, it is the weakness, then," said the doctor. "I will do all that science, so far as it may filter through my efforts, can accomplish. But whenever my patient begins to count the carriages in her funeral procession I subtract 50 per cent. from the curative power of medicines. If you will get her to ask one question about the new winter styles in cloak sleeves I will promise you a one-in-five chance for her, instead of one in ten."

After the doctor had gone Sue went into the workroom and cried a Japanese napkin to a pulp. Then she swaggered into Johnsy's room with her drawing board, whistling ragtime.

Johnsy lay, scarcely making a ripple under the bedclothes, with her face toward the window. Sue stopped whistling, thinking she was asleep.

She arranged her board and began a pen-and-ink drawing to illustrate a magazine story. Young artists must pave their way to Art by drawing pictures for magazine stories that young authors write to pave their way to Literature.

As Sue was sketching a pair of elegant horseshow riding trousers and a monocle on the figure of the hero, an Idaho cowboy, she heard a low sound, several times repeated. She went quickly to the bedside.

Johnsy's eyes were open wide. She was looking out the window and counting—counting backward.

"Twelve," she said, and a little later "eleven"; and then "ten," and "nine"; and then "eight" and "seven," almost together.

Sue looked solicitously out the window. What was there to count? There was only a bare, dreary yard to be seen, and the blank side of the brick house twenty feet away. An old, old ivy vine, gnarled and decayed at the roots, climbed half way up the brick wall. The cold breath of autumn had stricken its leaves from the vine until its skeleton branches clung, almost bare, to the crumbling bricks.

"What is it, dear?" asked Sue.

"Six," said Johnsy, in almost a whisper. "They're falling faster now. Three days ago there were almost a hundred. It made my head ache to count them. But now it's easy. There goes another one. There are only five left now."

"Five what, dear? Tell your Sudie."

"Leaves. On the ivy vine. When the last one falls I must go, too. I've known that for three days. Didn't the doctor tell you?"

"Oh, I never heard of such nonsense," complained Sue, with magnificent scorn. "What have old ivy leaves to do with your getting well? And you used to love that vine so, you naughty girl. Don't be a goosey. Why, the doctor told me this morning that your chances for getting well real soon were—let's see exactly what he said—he said the chances were ten to one! Why, that's almost as good a chance as we have in New York when we ride on the street cars or walk past a new building. Try to take some broth now, and let Sudie go back to her drawing, so she can sell the editor man with it, and buy port wine for her sick child, and pork chops for her greedy self."

"You needn't get any more wine," said Johnsy, keeping her eyes fixed out the window. "There goes another. No, I don't want any broth. That leaves just four. I want to see the last one fall before it gets dark. Then I'll go, too."

"Johnsy, dear," said Sue, bending over her, "will you promise me to keep your eyes closed, and not look out the window until I am done working? I must hand those drawings in by tomorrow. I need the light, or I would draw the shade down."

"Couldn't you draw in the other room?" asked Johnsy, coldly.

"I'd rather be here by you," said Sue. "Besides, I don't want you to keep looking at those silly ivy leaves."

"Tell me as soon as you have finished," said Johnsy, closing her eyes, and lying white and still as a fallen statue, "because I want to see the last one fall. I'm tired of waiting. I'm tired of thinking. I want to turn loose my hold on everything, and go sailing down, down, just like one of those poor, tired leaves."

"Try to sleep," said Sue. "I must call Behrman up to be my model for the old hermit miner. I'll not be gone a minute. Don't try to move 'till I come back."

Old Behrman was a painter who lived on the ground floor beneath them. He was past sixty and had a Michael Angelo's Moses† beard curling down from the head of a satyr along the body of an imp. Behrman was a failure in art. Forty years he had wielded the brush without getting near enough to touch the hem of his Mistress's robe.† He had been always about to paint a masterpiece, but had never yet begun it. For several years he had painted nothing except now and then a daub in the line of commerce or advertising. He earned a littl'e by serving as a model to those young artists in the colony who could not pay the price of a professional. He drank gin to excess, and still talked of his coming masterpiece. For the rest he was a fierce little old man, who scoffed terribly at softness in any one, and who regarded himself as especial mastiff-in-waiting to protect the two young artists in the studio above.

Sue found Behrman smelling strongly of juniper berries† in his dimly lighted den below. In one corner was a blank canvas on an easel that had been waiting there for twenty-five years to receive the first line of the masterpiece. She told him of Johnsy's fancy, and how she feared she would, indeed, light and fragile as a leaf herself, float away when her slight hold upon the world grew weaker.

Old Behrman, with his red eyes plainly streaming, shouted his contempt and derision for such idiotic imaginings.

"Vass!"† he cried. "Is dere people in de world mit der foolishness to die because leafs dey drop off from a confounded vine? I haf not heard of such a thing. No, I will not bose as a model for your fool hermit-dunderhead. Vy do you allow dot silly pusiness to come in der prain of her? Ach, dot poor leetle Miss Yohnsy."

"She is very ill and weak," said Sue, "and the fever has left her mind morbid and full of strange fancies. Very well, Mr. Behrman, if you do not care to pose for me, you needn't. But I think you are a horrid old—old flibbertigibbet."

"You are just like a woman!" yelled Behrman. "Who said I will not bose? Go on. I come mit you. For half an hour I haf peen trying to say dot I am ready to bose. Gott!† dis is not any blace in which one so goot as Miss Yohnsy shall lie sick. Some day I vill baint a masterpiece, and ve shall all go away. Gott! yes."

Johnsy was sleeping when they went upstairs. Sue pulled the shade down to the window-sill, and motioned Behrman into the other room. In there they peered out the window fearfully at the ivy vine. Then they looked at each other for a moment without speaking. A persistent, cold rain was falling, mingled with snow. Behrman, in his old blue shirt, took his seat as the hermit miner on an upturned kettle for a rock.

When Sue awoke from an hour's sleep the next morning she found Johnsy with dull, wide-open eyes staring at the drawn green shade.

"Pull it up; I want to see," she ordered, in a whisper.

Wearily Sue obeyed.

But, lo! after the beating rain and fierce gusts of wind that had endured through the livelong night, there yet stood out against the brick wall one ivy leaf. It was the last on the vine. Still dark green near its stem, but with its serrated edges tinted with the yellow of dissolution and decay, it hung bravely from a branch some twenty feet above the ground.

"It is the last one," said Johnsy. "I thought it would surely fall during the night. I heard the wind. It will fall to-day, and I shall die at the same time."

"Dear, dear!" said Sue, leaning her worn face down to the pillow, "think of me, if you won't think of yourself. What would I do?"

But Johnsy did not answer. The lonesomest thing in all the world is a soul when it is making ready to go on its mysterious, far journey. The fancy seemed to possess her more strongly as one by one the ties that bound her to friendship and to earth were loosed.

The day wore away, and even through the twilight they could see the lone ivy leaf clinging to its stem against the wall. And then, with the coming of the night the north wind was again loosed, while the rain still beat against the windows and pattered down from the low Dutch eaves.

When it was light enough Johnsy, the merciless, commanded that the shade be raised.

The ivy leaf was still there.

Johnsy lay for a long time looking at it. And then she called to Sue, who was stirring her chicken broth over the gas stove.

"I've been a bad girl, Sudie," said Johnsy. "Something has made that last leaf stay there to show me how wicked I was. It is a sin to want to die. You may bring me a little broth now, and some milk with a little port in it, and—no; bring me a hand-mirror first, and then pack some pillows about me, and I will sit up and watch you cook."

An hour later she said:

"Sudie, some day I hope to paint the Bay of Naples."

The doctor came in the afternoon, and Sue had an excuse to go into the hallway as he left.

"Even chances," said the doctor, taking Sue's thin, shaking hand in his. "With good nursing you'll win. And now I must see another case I have downstairs. Behrman, his name is—some kind of an artist, I believe. Pneumonia, too. He is an old, weak man, and the attack is acute. There is no hope for him; but he goes to the hospital to-day to be made more comfortable."

The next day the doctor said to Sue: "She's out of danger. You've won. Nutrition and care now—that's all."

And that afternoon Sue came to the bed where Johnsy lay, contentedly knitting a very blue and very useless woolen shoulder scarf, and put one arm around her, pillows and all.

"I have something to tell you, white mouse," she said. "Mr. Behrman died of pneumonia to-day in the hospital. He was ill only two days. The janitor found him on the morning of the first day in his room downstairs helpless with pain. His shoes and clothing were wet through and icy cold. They couldn't imagine where he had been on such a dreadful night. And then they found a lantern, still lighted, and a ladder that had been dragged from its place, and some scattered brushes, and a palette with green and yellow colors mixed on it, and—look out the window, dear, at the last ivy leaf on the wall. Didn't you wonder why it never fluttered or moved when the wind blew? Ah, darling, it's Behrman's masterpiece—he painted it there the night that the last leaf fell."

The Gift of the Magi

ONE DOLLAR AND eighty-seven cents. That was all. And sixty cents of it was in pennies.† Pennies saved one and two at a time by bulldozing the grocer and the vegetable man and the butcher until one's cheeks burned with the silent imputation of parsimony that such close dealing implied. Three times Della counted it. One dollar and eighty-seven cents. And the next day would be Christmas.

There was clearly nothing to do but flop down on the shabby little couch and howl. So Della did it. Which instigates the moral reflection that life is made up of sobs, sniffles, and smiles,† with sniffles predominating.

While the mistress of the home is gradually subsiding from the first stage to the second, take a look at the home. A furnished flat at $8 per week.† It did not exactly beggar description, but it certainly had that word on the lookout for the mendicancy squad.

In the vestibule below was a letter-box into which no letter would go, and an electric button from which no mortal finger could coax a ring. Also appertaining thereunto was a card bearing the name "Mr. James Dillingham Young." The "Dillingham" had been flung to the breeze during a former period of prosperity when its possessor was being paid $30 per week. Now, when the income was shrunk to $20, the letters of "Dillingham" looked blurred, as though they were thinking seriously of contracting to a modest and unassuming D. But whenever Mr. James Dillingham Young came home and reached his flat above he was called "Jim" and greatly hugged by Mrs.

James Dillingham Young, already introduced to you as Della. Which is all very good.

Della finished her cry and attended to her cheeks with the powder rag. She stood by the window and looked out dully at a grey cat walking a grey fence in a grey backyard. Tomorrow would be Christmas Day, and she had only $1.87 with which to buy Jim a present. She had been saving every penny she could for months, with this result. Twenty dollars a week doesn't go far. Expenses had been greater than she had calculated. They always are. Only $1.87 to buy a present for Jim. Her Jim. Many a happy hour she had spent planning for something nice for him. Something fine and rare and sterling—something just a little bit near to being worthy of the honor of being owned by Jim.

There was a pier-glass between the windows of the room. Perhaps you have seen a pier-glass in an $8 flat. A very thin and very agile person may, by observing his reflection in a rapid sequence of longitudinal strips, obtain a fairly accurate conception of his looks. Della, being slender, had mastered the art.

Suddenly she whirled from the window and stood before the glass. Her eyes were shining brilliantly, but her face had lost its color within twenty seconds. Rapidly she pulled down her hair and let it fall to its full length.

Now, there were two possessions of the James Dillingham Youngs in which they both took a mighty pride. One was Jim's gold watch that had been his father's and his grandfather's. The other was Della's hair. Had the Queen of Sheba[†] lived in the flat across the airshaft, Della would have let her hair hang out the window some day to dry just to depreciate Her Majesty's jewels and gifts. Had King Solomon[†] been the janitor, with all his treasures piled up in the basement, Jim would have pulled out his watch every time he passed, just to see him pluck at his beard from envy.

So now Della's beautiful hair fell about her, rippling and shining like a cascade of brown waters. It reached below her knee and made itself almost a garment for her. And then she did it up again nervously and quickly. Once she faltered for a minute and stood still while a tear or two splashed on the worn red carpet.

On went her old brown jacket; on went her old brown hat. With a whirl of skirts and with the brilliant sparkle still in her eyes, she fluttered out the door and down the stairs to the street.

Where she stopped the sign read: "Mme. Sofronie. Hair Goods of All Kinds." One flight up Della ran, and collected herself, panting. Madame, large, too white, chilly, hardly looked the "Sofronie."

"Will you buy my hair?" asked Della.

"I buy hair," said Madame. "Take yer hat off and let's have a sight at the looks of it."

Down rippled the brown cascade. "Twenty dollars," said Madame, lifting the mass with a practised hand.

"Give it to me quick," said Della.

Oh, and the next two hours tripped by on rosy wings. Forget the hashed metaphor. She was ransacking the stores for Jim's present.

She found it at last. It surely had been made for Jim and no one else. There was no other like it in any of the stores, and she had turned all of them inside out. It was a platinum fob chain simple and chaste in design, properly proclaiming its value by substance alone and not by meretricious ornamentation—as all good things should do. It was even worthy of The Watch. As soon as she saw it she knew that it must be Jim's. It was like him. Quietness and value—the description applied to both. Twenty-one dollars they took from her for it, and she hurried home with the 87 cents. With that chain on his watch Jim might be properly anxious about the time in any company. Grand as the watch was, he sometimes looked at it on the sly on account of the old leather strap that he used in place of a chain.

When Della reached home her intoxication gave way a little to prudence and reason. She got out her curling irons and lighted the gas and went to work repairing the ravages made by generosity added to love. Which is always a tremendous task, dear friends—a mammoth task.

Within forty minutes her head was covered with tiny, close-lying curls that made her look wonderfully like a truant schoolboy. She looked at her reflection in the mirror long, carefully, and critically.

"If Jim doesn't kill me," she said to herself, "before he takes a second look at me, he'll say I look like a Coney Island† chorus girl. But what could I do—oh! what could I do with a dollar and eighty-seven cents?"

At 7 o'clock the coffee was made and the frying-pan was on the back of the stove hot and ready to cook the chops.

Jim was never late. Della doubled the fob chain in her hand and sat on the corner of the table near the door that he always entered. Then she heard his step on the stair away down on the first flight, and she turned white for just a moment. She had a habit for saying little silent prayers about the simplest everyday things, and now she whispered: "Please God, make him think I am still pretty."

The door opened and Jim stepped in and closed it. He looked thin and very serious. Poor fellow, he was only twenty-two—and to be burdened with a family! He needed a new overcoat and he was without gloves.

Jim stopped inside the door, as immovable as a setter at the scent of quail. His eyes were fixed upon Della, and there was an expression in them that she could not read, and it terrified her. It was not anger, nor surprise, nor disapproval, nor horror, nor any of the sentiments that she had been prepared for. He simply stared at her fixedly with that peculiar expression on his face.

Della wriggled off the table and went for him.

"Jim, darling," she cried, "don't look at me that way. I had my hair cut off and sold it because I couldn't have lived through Christmas without giving you a present. It'll grow out again—you won't mind, will you? I just had to do it. My hair grows awfully fast. Say 'Merry Christmas!' Jim, and let's be happy. You don't know what a nice—what a beautiful, nice gift I've got for you."

"You've cut off your hair?" asked Jim, laboriously, as if he had not arrived at that patent fact yet even after the hardest mental labor.

"Cut it off and sold it," said Della. "Don't you like me just as well, anyhow? I'm me without my hair, ain't I?"

Jim looked about the room curiously.

"You say your hair is gone?" he said, with an air almost of idiocy.

"You needn't look for it," said Della. "It's sold, I tell you—sold and gone, too. It's Christmas Eve, boy. Be good to me, for it went for you. Maybe the hairs of my head were numbered," she went on with sudden serious sweetness, "but nobody could ever count my love for you. Shall I put the chops on, Jim?"

Out of his trance Jim seemed quickly to wake. He enfolded his Della. For ten seconds let us regard with discreet scrutiny some inconsequential object in the other direction. Eight dollars a week or a million a year—what is the difference? A mathematician or a wit would give you the wrong answer. The magi brought valuable gifts,† but that was not among them. This dark assertion will be illuminated later on.

Jim drew a package from his overcoat pocket and threw it upon the table.

"Don't make any mistake, Dell," he said, "about me. I don't think there's anything in the way of a haircut or a shave or a shampoo that could make me like my girl any less. But if you'll unwrap that package you may see why you had me going a while at first."

White fingers and nimble tore at the string and paper. And then an ecstatic scream of joy; and then, alas! a quick feminine change to hysterical tears and wails, necessitating the immediate employment of all the comforting powers of the lord of the flat.

For there lay The Combs—the set of combs, side and back, that Della had worshipped long in a Broadway window. Beautiful combs, pure tortoise shell, with jewelled rims—just the shade to wear in the beautiful vanished hair. They were expensive combs, she knew, and her heart had simply craved and yearned over them without the least hope of possession. And now, they were hers, but the tresses that should have adorned the coveted adornments were gone.

But she hugged them to her bosom, and at length she was able to look up with dim eyes and a smile and say: "My hair grows so fast, Jim!"

And them Della leaped up like a little singed cat and cried, "Oh, oh!"

Jim had not yet seen his beautiful present. She held it out to him eagerly upon her open palm. The dull precious metal seemed to flash with a reflection of her bright and ardent spirit.

"Isn't it a dandy, Jim? I hunted all over town to find it. You'll have to look at the time a hundred times a day now. Give me your watch. I want to see how it looks on it."

Instead of obeying, Jim tumbled down on the couch and put his hands under the back of his head and smiled.

"Dell," said he, "let's put our Christmas presents away and keep 'em a while. They're too nice to use just at present. I sold the watch to get the money to buy your combs. And now suppose you put the chops on."

The magi, as you know, were wise men—wonderfully wise men—who brought gifts to the Babe in the manger. They invented the art of giving Christmas presents. Being wise, their gifts were no doubt wise ones, possibly bearing the privilege of exchange in case of duplication. And here I have lamely related to you the uneventful chronicle of two foolish children in a flat who most unwisely sacrificed for each other the greatest treasures of their house. But in a last word to the wise of these days let it be said that of all who give gifts these two were the wisest.[†] Of all who give and receive gifts, such as they are wisest. Everywhere they are wisest. They are the magi.

The Cop and the Anthem

On his bench in Madison Square Soapy moved uneasily. When wild geese honk high of nights, and when women without sealskin coats grow kind to their husbands, and when Soapy moves uneasily on his bench in the park, you may know that winter is near at hand.

A dead leaf fell in Soapy's lap. That was Jack Frost's card. Jack is kind to the regular denizens of Madison Square, and gives fair warning of his annual call. At the corners of four streets he hands his pasteboard to the North Wind, footman of the mansion of All Outdoors, so that the inhabitants thereof may make ready.

Soapy's mind became cognizant of the fact that the time had come for him to resolve himself into a singular Committee of Ways and Means to provide against the coming rigor. And therefore he moved uneasily on his bench.

The hibernatorial ambitions of Soapy were not of the highest. In them there were no considerations of Mediterranean cruises, of soporific Southern skies drifting in the Vesuvian Bay.† Three months on the Island was what his soul craved. Three months of assured board and bed and congenial company, safe from Boreas and bluecoats,† seemed to Soapy the essence of things desirable.

For years the hospitable Blackwell's had been his winter quarters. Just as his more fortunate fellow New Yorkers had bought their tickets to Palm

Beach† and the Riviera† each winter, so Soapy had made his humble arrangements for his annual hegira to the Island. And now the time was come. On the previous night three Sabbath† newspapers, distributed beneath his coat, about his ankles and over his lap, had failed to repulse the cold as he slept on his bench near the spurting fountain in the ancient square. So the Island loomed big and timely in Soapy's mind. He scorned the provisions made in the name of charity for the city's dependents. In Soapy's opinion the Law was more benign than Philanthropy. There was an endless round of institutions, municipal and eleemosynary, on which he might set out and receive lodging and food accordant with the simple life. But to one of Soapy's proud spirit the gifts of charity are encumbered. If not in coin you must pay in humiliation of spirit for every benefit received at the hands of philanthropy. As Caesar had his Brutus,† every bed of charity must have its toll of a bath, every loaf of bread its compensation of a private and personal inquisition. Wherefore it is better to be a guest of the law, which though conducted by rules, does not meddle unduly with a gentleman's private affairs.

Soapy, having decided to go to the Island, at once set about accomplishing his desire. There were many easy ways of doing this. The pleasantest was to dine luxuriously at some expensive restaurant; and then, after declaring insolvency, be handed over quietly and without uproar to a policeman. An accommodating magistrate would do the rest.

Soapy left his bench and strolled out of the square and across the level sea of asphalt, where Broadway and Fifth Avenue flow together. Up Broadway he turned, and halted at a glittering café, where are gathered together nightly the choicest products of the grape, the silkworm and the protoplasm.†

Soapy had confidence in himself from the lowest button of his vest upward. He was shaven, and his coat was decent and his neat black, ready-tied four-in-hand† had been presented to him by a lady missionary on Thanksgiving Day. If he could reach a table in the restaurant unsuspected success would be his. The portion of him that would show above the table would raise no doubt in the waiter's mind. A roasted mallard duck, thought Soapy, would be about the thing—with a bottle of Chablis, and then Camembert, a demitasse and a cigar. One dollar for the cigar would be enough. The total would not be so high as to call forth any supreme manifestation of revenge from the café management; and yet the meat would leave him filled and happy for the journey to his winter refuge.

But as Soapy set foot inside the restaurant door the head waiter's eye fell upon his frayed trousers and decadent shoes. Strong and ready hands turned him about and conveyed him in silence and haste to the sidewalk and averted the ignoble fate of the menaced mallard.

Soapy turned off Broadway. It seemed that his route to the coveted island was not to be an epicurean one. Some other way of entering limbo must be thought of.

At a corner of Sixth Avenue electric lights and cunningly displayed wares behind plate-glass made a shop window conspicuous. Soapy took a cobblestone and dashed it through the glass. People came running around the corner, a policeman in the lead. Soapy stood still, with his hands in his pockets, and smiled at the sight of brass buttons.

"Where's the man that done that?" inquired the officer excitedly.

"Don't you figure out that I might have had something to do with it?" said Soapy, not without sarcasm, but friendly, as one greets good fortune.

The policeman's mind refused to accept Soapy even as a clue. Men who smash windows do not remain to parley with the law's minions. They take to their heels. The policeman saw a man half way down the block running to catch a car. With drawn club he joined in the pursuit. Soapy, with disgust in his heart, loafed along, twice unsuccessful.

On the opposite side of the street was a restaurant of no great pretensions. It catered to large appetites and modest purses. Its crockery and atmosphere were thick; its soup and napery thin. Into this place Soapy took his accusive shoes and telltale trousers without challenge. At a table he sat and consumed beefsteak, flapjacks, doughnuts and pie. And then to the waiter he betrayed the fact that the minutest coin and himself were strangers.

"Now, get busy and call a cop," said Soapy. "And don't keep a gentleman waiting."

"No cops for youse," said the waiter, with a voice like butter cakes and an eye like the cherry in a Manhattan cocktail. "Hey, Con!"

Neatly upon his left ear on the callous pavement two waiters pitched Soapy. He arose, joint by joint, as a carpenter's rule opens, and beat the dust from his clothes. Arrest seemed but a rosy dream. The Island seemed very far away. A policeman who stood before a drug store two doors away laughed and walked down the street.

Five blocks Soapy traveled before his courage permitted him to woo capture again. This time the opportunity presented what he fatuously termed to himself a "cinch." A young woman of a modest and pleasing guise was standing before a show window gazing with sprightly interest at its display of shaving mugs and inkstands, and two yards from the window a large policeman of severe demeanor leaned against a water plug.

It was Soapy's design to assume the role of the despicable and execrated "masher."† The refined and elegant appearance of his victim and the contiguity of the conscientious cop encouraged him to believe that he would soon feel the pleasant official clutch upon his arm that would insure his winter quarters on the right little, tight little isle.

Soapy straightened the lady missionary's ready-made tie, dragged his shrinking cuffs into the open, set his hat at a killing cant and sidled toward the young woman. He made eyes at her, was taken with sudden coughs and "hems," smiled, smirked and went brazenly through the impudent and contemptible litany of the "masher." With half an eye Soapy saw that the policeman was watching him fixedly. The young woman moved away a few steps, and again bestowed her absorbed attention upon the shaving mugs. Soapy followed, boldly stepping to her side, raised his hat and said:

"Ah there, Bedelia! Don't you want to come and play in my yard?"

The policeman was still looking. The persecuted young woman had but to beckon a finger and Soapy would be practically en route for his insular haven. Already he imagined he could feel the cozy warmth of the station-house. The young woman faced him and, stretching out a hand, caught Soapy's coat sleeve.

"Sure, Mike," she said joyfully, "if you'll blow me to a pail of suds.† I'd have spoke to you sooner, but the cop was watching."

With the young woman playing the clinging ivy to his oak Soapy walked past the policeman overcome with gloom. He seemed doomed to liberty.†

At the next corner he shook off his companion and ran. He halted in the district where by night are found the lightest streets, hearts, vows and librettos. Women in furs and men in greatcoats moved gaily in the wintry air. A sudden fear seized Soapy that some dreadful enchantment had rendered him immune to arrest. The thought brought a little of panic upon it, and when he came upon another policeman lounging grandly in front of a transplendent theatre he caught at the immediate straw of "disorderly conduct."

On the sidewalk Soapy began to yell drunken gibberish at the top of his harsh voice. He danced, howled, raved and otherwise disturbed the welkin.

The policeman twirled his club, turned his back to Soapy and remarked to a citizen.

"'Tis one of them Yale lads celebratin' the goose egg they give to the Hartford College. Noisy; but no harm. We've instructions to lave them be."

Disconsolate, Soapy ceased his unavailing racket. Would never a police man lay hands on him? In his fancy the Island seemed an unattainable Arcadia.† He buttoned his thin coat against the chilling wind.

In a cigar store he saw a well-dressed man lighting a cigar at a swinging light. His silk umbrella he had set by the door on entering. Soapy stepped inside, secured the umbrella and sauntered off with it slowly. The man at the cigar light followed hastily.

"My umbrella," he said, sternly.

"Oh, is it?" sneered Soapy, adding insult to petit larceny. "Well, why don't you call a policeman? I took it. Your umbrella! Why don't you call a cop? There stands one on the corner."

The umbrella owner slowed his steps. Soapy did likewise, with a presentiment that luck would again run against him. The policeman looked at the two curiously.

"Of course," said the umbrella man—"that is—well, you know how these mistakes occur—I—if it's your umbrella I hope you'll excuse me—I picked it up this morning in a restaurant—If you recognize it as yours, why—I hope you'll—"

"Of course it's mine," said Soapy, viciously.

The ex-umbrella man retreated. The policeman hurried to assist a tall blonde in an opera cloak across the street in front of a street car that was approaching two blocks away.

Soapy walked eastward through a street damaged by improvements. He hurled the umbrella wrathfully into an excavation. He muttered against the men who wear helmets and carry clubs. Because he wanted to fall into their clutches, they seemed to regard him as a king who could do no wrong.

At length Soapy reached one of the avenues to the east where the glitter and turmoil was but faint. He set his face down this toward Madison Square, for the homing instinct survives even when the home is a park bench.

But on an unusually quiet corner Soapy came to a standstill. Here was an old church, quaint and rambling and gabled. Through one violet-stained window a soft light glowed, where, no doubt, the organist loitered over the keys, making sure of his mastery of the coming Sabbath anthem. For there drifted out to Soapy's ears sweet music that caught and held him transfixed against the convolutions of the iron fence.

The moon was above, lustrous and serene; vehicles and pedestrians were few; sparrows twittered sleepily in the eaves—for a little while the scene might have been a country churchyard. And the anthem that the organist played cemented Soapy to the iron fence, for he had known it well in the days when his life contained such things as mothers and roses and ambitions and friends and immaculate thoughts and collars.

The conjunction of Soapy's receptive state of mind and the influences about the old church wrought a sudden and wonderful change in his soul. He viewed with swift horror the pit into which he had tumbled, the degraded days, unworthy desires, dead hopes, wrecked faculties and base motives that made up his existence.

And also in a moment his heart responded thrillingly to this novel mood. An instantaneous and strong impulse moved him to battle with his desperate fate. He would pull himself out of the mire; he would make a man of himself again; he would conquer the evil that had taken possession of him. There was time; he was comparatively young yet; he would resurrect his old eager ambitions and pursue them without faltering. Those solemn but sweet organ notes had set up a revolution in him. Tomorrow he would go into the roaring downtown district and find work. A fur importer had once offered him a place as driver. He would find him tomorrow and ask for the position. He would be somebody in the world. He would—

Soapy felt a hand laid on his arm. He looked quickly around into the broad face of a policeman.

"What are you doin' here?" asked the officer.

"Nothin'," said Soapy.

"Then come along," said the policeman.

"Three months on the Island," said the Magistrate† in the Police Court the next morning.

The Green Door

SUPPOSE YOU SHOULD be walking down Broadway after dinner, with ten minutes allotted to the consummation of your cigar while you are choosing between a diverting tragedy and something serious in the way of vaudeville.† Suddenly a hand is laid upon your arm. You turn to look into the thrilling eyes of a beautiful woman, wonderful in diamonds and Russian sables.† She thrusts hurriedly into your hand an extremely hot buttered roll, flashes out a tiny pair of scissors, snips off the second button of your overcoat, meaningly ejaculates the one word, "parallelogram!" and swiftly flies down a cross street, looking back fearfully over her shoulder.

That would be pure adventure. Would you accept it? Not you. You would flush with embarrassment; you would sheepishly drop the roll and continue down Broadway, fumbling feebly for the missing button. This you would do unless you are one of the blessed few in whom the pure spirit of adventure is not dead.

True adventurers have never been plentiful. They who are set down in print as such have been mostly business men with newly invented methods. They have been out after the things they wanted—golden fleeces, holy grails,† lady loves, treasure, crowns and fame. The true adventurer goes forth aimless and uncalculating to meet and greet unknown fate. A fine example was the Prodigal Son†—when he started back home.

Half-adventurers—brave and splendid figures—have been numerous. From the Crusades to the Palisades† they have enriched the arts of history and fiction and the trade of historical fiction. But each of them had a prize to win, a goal to kick, an axe to grind, a race to run, a new thrust in tierce to deliver, a name to carve, a crow to pick—so they were not followers of true adventure.

In the big city the twin spirits Romance and Adventure are always abroad seeking worthy wooers. As we roam the streets they slyly peep at us and challenge us in twenty different guises. Without knowing why, we look up suddenly to see in a window a face that seems to belong to our gallery of intimate portraits; in a sleeping thoroughfare we hear a cry of agony and fear coming from an empty and shuttered house; instead of at our familiar curb a cab-driver deposits us before a strange door, which one, with a smile, opens for us and bids us enter; a slip of paper, written upon, flutters down to our feet from the high lattices of Chance; we exchange glances of instantaneous hate, affection and fear with hurrying strangers in the passing crowds; a sudden souse of rain—and our umbrella may be sheltering the daughter of the Full Moon and first cousin of the Sidereal System;† at every corner handkerchiefs drop, fingers beckon, eyes besiege, and the lost, the lonely, the rapturous, the mysterious, the perilous changing clues of adventure are slipped into our fingers. But few of us are willing to hold and follow them. We are grown stiff with the ramrod of convention down our backs. We pass on; and some day we come, at the end of a very dull life, to reflect that our romance has been a pallid thing of a marriage or two, a satin rosette kept in a safe-deposit drawer, and a lifelong feud with a steam radiator.

Rudolf Steiner was a true adventurer. Few were the evenings on which he did not go forth from his hall bedchamber in search of the unexpected and the egregious. The most interesting thing in life seemed to him to be what might lie just around the next corner. Sometimes his willingness to tempt fate led him into strange paths. Twice he had spent the night in a station-house; again and again he had found himself the dupe of ingenious and mercenary tricksters; his watch and money had been the price of one flattering allurement. But with undiminished ardor he picked up every glove cast before him into the merry lists of adventure.

One evening Rudolf was strolling along a cross-town street in the older central part of the city. Two streams of people filled the sidewalks—the home-hurrying, and that restless contingent that abandons home for the specious welcome of the thousand-candle-power *table d'hôte*.

The young adventurer was of pleasing presence, and moved serenely and watchfully. By daylight he was a salesman in a piano store. He wore his tie drawn through a topaz ring instead of fastened with a stick pin; and once he had written to the editor of a magazine that "Junie's Love Test" by Miss Libbey,† had been the book that had most influenced his life.

During his walk a violent chattering of teeth in a glass case on the sidewalk seemed at first to draw his attention (with a qualm), to a restaurant before which it was set; but a second glance revealed the electric letters of a dentist's sign high above the next door. A giant Negro, fantastically dressed in a red embroidered coat, yellow trousers and a military cap, discreetly distributed cards to those of the passing crowd who consented to take them.

This mode of dentistic advertising was a common sight to Rudolf. Usually he passed the dispenser of the dentist's cards without reducing his store; but tonight the African slipped one into his hand so deftly that he retained it there smiling a little at the successful feat.

When he had traveled a few yards further he glanced at the card indifferently. Surprised, he turned it over and looked again with interest. One side of the card was blank; on the other was written in ink three words, "The Green Door." And then Rudolf saw, three steps in front of him, a man throw down the card the Negro had given him as he passed. Rudolf picked it up. It was printed with the dentist's name and address and the usual schedule of "plate work" and "bridge work" and "crowns," and specious promises of "painless" operations.

The adventurous piano salesman halted at the corner and considered. Then he crossed the street, walked down a block, recrossed and joined the upward current of people again. Without seeming to notice the Negro as he passed the second time, he carelessly took the card that was handed him. Ten steps away he inspected it. In the same handwriting that appeared on the first card "The Green Door" was inscribed upon it. Three or four cards were tossed to the pavement by pedestrians both following and leading him. These fell blank side up. Rudolf turned them over. Every one bore the printed legend of the dental "parlors."

Rarely did the arch sprite Adventure need to beckon twice to Rudolf Steiner, his true follower. But twice it had been done, and the quest was on.

Rudolf walked slowly back to where the giant Negro stood by the case of rattling teeth. This time as he passed he received no card. In spite of his gaudy and ridiculous garb, the Ethiopian displayed a natural barbaric dignity as he stood, offering the cards suavely to some, allowing others to pass unmolested. Every half minute he chanted a harsh, unintelligible phrase akin to the jabber of car conductors and grand opera. And not only did he withhold a card this time, but it seemed to Rudolf that he received from the shining and massive black countenance a look of cold, almost contemptuous disdain.

The look stung the adventurer. He read in it a silent accusation that he had been found wanting. Whatever the mysterious written words on the cards might mean, the black had selected him twice from the throng for their recipient; and now seemed to have condemned him as deficient in the wit and spirit to engage the enigma.

Standing aside from the rush, the young man made a rapid estimate of the building in which he conceived that his adventure must lie. Five stories high it rose. A small restaurant occupied the basement.

The first floor, now closed, seemed to house millinery or furs. The second floor, by the winking electric letters, was the dentist's. Above this a polyglot babel of signs struggled to indicate the abodes of palmists, dressmakers, musicians and doctors. Still higher up draped curtains and milk bottles white on the window sills proclaimed the regions of domesticity.

After concluding his survey Rudolf walked briskly up the high flight of stone steps into the house. Up two flights of the carpeted stairway he continued; and at its top paused. The hallway there was dimly lighted by two pale jets of gas—one far to his right, the other nearer, to his left. He looked toward the nearer light and saw, within its wan halo, a green door. For one moment he hesitated; then he seemed to see the contumelious sneer of the African juggler of cards; and then he walked straight to the green door and knocked against it.

Moments like those that passed before his knock was answered measure the quick breath of true adventure. What might not be behind those green panels! Gamesters at play; cunning rogues baiting their traps with subtle skill; beauty in love with courage, and thus planning to be sought by it; danger, death, love, disappointment, ridicule—any of these might respond to that temerarious rap.

A faint rustle was heard inside, and the door slowly opened. A girl not yet twenty stood there, white-faced and tottering. She loosed the knob and swayed weakly, groping with one hand. Rudolf caught her and laid her on a faded couch that stood against the wall. He closed the door and took a swift glance around the room by the light of a flickering gas jet. Neat, but extreme poverty was the story that he read.

The girl lay still, as if in a faint. Rudolf looked around the room excitedly for a barrel. People must be rolled upon a barrel who—no, no; that was for drowned persons. He began to fan her with his hat. That was successful, for he struck her nose with the brim of his derby and she opened her eyes.

And then the young man saw that hers, indeed, was the one missing face from his heart's gallery of intimate portraits. The frank, grey eyes, the little nose, turning pertly outward; the chestnut hair, curling like the tendrils of a pea vine, seemed the right end and reward of all his wonderful adventures. But the face was woefully thin and pale.

The girl looked at him calmly, and then smiled.

"Fainted, didn't I?" she asked, weakly. "Well, who wouldn't? You try going without anything to eat for three days and see!"

"Himmel!"† exclaimed Rudolf, jumping up. "Wait till I come back."

He dashed out the green door and down the stairs. In twenty minutes he was back again, kicking at the door with his toe for her to open it. With both arms he hugged an array of wares from the grocery and the restaurant. On the table he laid them—bread and butter, cold meats, cakes, pies, pickles, oysters, a roasted chicken, a bottle of milk and one of red-hot tea.

"This is ridiculous," said Rudolf, blusteringly, "to go without eating. You must quit making election bets of this kind. Supper is ready." He helped her to a chair at the table and asked: "Is there a cup for the tea?" "On the shelf by the window," she answered. When he turned again with the cup he saw her, with eyes shining rapturously, beginning upon a huge Dill pickle that she had rooted out from the paper bags with a woman's unerring instinct. He took it from her, laughingly, and poured the cup full of milk. "Drink that first," he ordered, "and then you shall have some tea, and then a chicken wing. If you are very good you shall have a pickle tomorrow. And now, if you'll allow me to be your guest we'll have supper."

He drew up the other chair. The tea brightened the girl's eyes and brought back some of her color. She began to eat with a sort of dainty ferocity like some starved wild animal. She seemed to regard the young man's presence and the aid he had rendered her as a natural thing—not as though she undervalued the conventions; but as one whose great stress gave her the right to put aside the artificial for the human. But gradually, with the return of strength and comfort, came also a sense of the little conventions that belong; and she began to tell him her little story. It was one of a thousand such as the city yawns at every day—the shop girl's story of insufficient wages, further reduced by "fines" that go to swell the store's profits; of time lost through illness; and then of lost positions, lost hope, and—the knock of the adventurer upon the green door.

But to Rudolf the history sounded as big as the Iliad† or the crisis in "Junie's Love Test."

"To think of you going through all that," he exclaimed.

"It was something fierce," said the girl, solemnly.

"And you have no relatives or friends in the city?"

"None whatever."

"I am all alone in the world, too," said Rudolf, after a pause.

"I am glad of that," said the girl, promptly; and somehow it pleased the young man to hear that she approved of his bereft condition.

Very suddenly her eyelids dropped and she sighed deeply.

"I'm awfully sleepy," she said, "and I feel so good."

Then Rudolf rose and took his hat. "I'll say good-night. A long night's sleep will be fine for you."

He held out his hand, and she took it and said "good-night." But her eyes asked a question so eloquently, so frankly and pathetically that he answered it with words.

"Oh, I'm coming back tomorrow to see how you are getting along. You can't get rid of me so easily."

Then, at the door, as though the way of his coming had been so much less important than the fact that he had come, she asked: "How did you come to knock at my door?"

He looked at her for a moment, remembering the cards, and felt a sudden jealous pain. What if they had fallen into other hands as adventurous as his? Quickly he decided that she must never know the truth. He would never let her know that he was aware of the strange expedient to which she had been driven by her great distress.

"One of our piano tuners lives in this house," he said. "I knocked at your door by mistake."

The last thing he saw in the room before the green door closed was her smile.

At the head of the stairway he paused and looked curiously about him. And then he went along the hallway to its other end; and, coming back, ascended to the floor above and continued his puzzled explorations. Every door that he found in the house was painted green.

Wondering, he descended to the sidewalk. The fantastic African was still there. Rudolf confronted him with his two cards in his hand.

"Will you tell me why you gave me these cards and what they mean?" he asked.

In a broad, good-natured grin the Negro exhibited a splendid advertisement of his master's profession.

"Dar it is, boss," he said, pointing down the street. "But I 'spect you is a little late for de fust act."

Looking the way he pointed Rudolf saw above the entrance to a theatre the blazing electric sign of its new play, "The Green Door."

"I'm informed dat it's a fust-rate show, sah," said the Negro. "De agent what represents it pussented me with a dollar, sah, to distribute a few of his cards along with de doctah's. May I offer you one of de doctah's cards, sah?"

At the corner of the block in which he lived Rudolf stopped for a glass of beer and a cigar. When he had come out with his lighted weed he buttoned his coat, pushed back his hat and said, stoutly, to the lamp post on the corner:

"All the same, I believe it was the hand of Fate that doped out the way for me to find her."

Which conclusion, under the circumstances, certainly admits Rudolf Steiner to the ranks of the true followers of Romance and Adventure.

After Twenty Years

THE POLICEMAN ON the beat moved up the avenue impressively. The impressiveness was habitual and not for show, for spectators were few. The time was barely 10 o'clock at night, but chilly gusts of wind with a taste of rain in them had well nigh depeopled the streets.

Trying doors as he went, twirling his club with many intricate and artful movements, turning now and then to cast his watchful eye adown the pacific thoroughfare, the officer, with his stalwart form and slight swagger, made a fine picture of a guardian of the peace. The vicinity was one that kept early hours. Now and then you might see the lights of a cigar store or of an all-night lunch counter; but the majority of the doors belonged to business places that had long since been closed.

When about midway of a certain block the policeman suddenly slowed his walk. In the doorway of a darkened hardware store a man leaned, with an unlighted cigar in his mouth. As the policeman walked up to him the man spoke up quickly.

"It's all right, officer," he said, reassuringly. "I'm just waiting for a friend. It's an appointment made twenty years ago. Sounds a little funny to you, doesn't it? Well, I'll explain if you'd like to make certain it's all straight. About that long ago there used to be a restaurant where this store stands—'Big Joe' Brady's restaurant."

"Until five years ago," said the policeman. "It was torn down then."

The man in the doorway struck a match and lit his cigar. The light showed a pale, square-jawed face with keen eyes, and a little white scar near his right eyebrow. His scarf pin was a large diamond, oddly set.

"Twenty years ago tonight," said the man, "I dined here at 'Big Joe' Brady's with Jimmy Wells, my best chum, and the finest chap in the world. He and I were raised here in New York, just like two brothers, together. I was eighteen and Jimmy was twenty. The next morning I was to start for the West to make my fortune. You couldn't have dragged Jimmy out of New York; he thought it was the only place on earth. Well, we agreed that night that we would meet here again exactly twenty years from that date and time, no matter what our conditions might be or from what distance we might have to come. We figured that in twenty years each of us ought to have our destiny worked out and our fortunes made, whatever they were going to be."

"It sounds pretty interesting," said the policeman. "Rather a long time between meets, though, it seems to me. Haven't you heard from your friend since you left?"

"Well, yes, for a time we corresponded," said the other. "But after a year or two we lost track of each other. You see, the West is a pretty big proposition, and I kept hustling around over it pretty lively. But I know Jimmy will meet me here if he's alive, for he always was the truest, staunchest old chap in the world. He'll never forget. I came a thousand miles to stand in this door tonight, and it's worth it if my old partner turns up."

The waiting man pulled out a handsome watch, the lids of it set with small diamonds.

"Three minutes to ten," he announced. "It was exactly ten o'clock when we parted here at the restaurant door."

"Did pretty well out West, didn't you?" asked the policeman.

"You bet! I hope Jimmy has done half as well. He was a kind of plodder, though, good fellow as he was. I've had to compete with some of the sharpest wits going to get my pile. A man gets in a groove in New York. It takes the West to put a razor-edge on him."

The policeman twirled his club and took a step or two.

"I'll be on my way. Hope your friend comes around all right. Going to call time on him sharp?"

"I should say not!" said the other. "I'll give him half an hour at least. If Jimmy is alive on earth he'll be here by that time. So long, officer."

"Good-night, sir," said the policeman, passing on along his beat, trying doors as he went.

There was now a fine, cold drizzle falling, and the wind had risen from its uncertain puffs into a steady blow. The few foot passengers astir in that quarter hurried dismally and silently along with coat collars turned high and pocketed hands. And in the door of the hardware store the man who had come a thousand miles to fill an appointment, uncertain almost to absurdity, with the friend of his youth, smoked his cigar and waited.

About twenty minutes he waited, and then a tall man in a long overcoat, with collar turned up to his ears, hurried across from the opposite side of the street. He went directly to the waiting man.

"Is that you, Bob?" he asked, doubtfully.

"Is that you, Jimmy Wells?" cried the man in the door.

"Bless my heart!" exclaimed the new arrival, grasping both the other's hands with his own. "It's Bob, sure as fate. I was certain I'd find you here if you were still in existence. Well, well, well!—twenty years is a long time. The old restaurant's gone, Bob; I wish it had lasted, so we could have had another dinner there. How has the West treated you, old man?"

"Bully;[†] it has given me everything I asked it for. You've changed lots, Jimmy. I never thought you were so tall by two or three inches."

"Oh, I grew a bit after I was twenty."

"Doing well in New York, Jimmy?"

"Moderately. I have a position in one of the city departments. Come on, Bob; we'll go around to a place I know of, and have a good long talk about old times."

The two men started up the street, arm in arm. The man from the West, his egotism enlarged by success, was beginning to outline the history of his career. The other, submerged in his overcoat, listened with interest.

At the corner stood a drug store, brilliant with electric lights. When they came into this glare each of them turned simultaneously to gaze upon the other's face.

The man from the West stopped suddenly and released his arm.

"You're not Jimmy Wells," he snapped. "Twenty years is a long time, but not long enough to change a man's nose from a Roman to a pug."

"It sometimes changes a good man into a bad one," said the tall man. "You've been under arrest for ten minutes, 'Silky' Bob. Chicago thinks you may have dropped over our way and wires us she wants to have a chat with you. Going quietly, are you? That's sensible. Now, before we go on to the station here's a note I was asked to hand you. You may read it here at the window. It's from Patrolman Wells."

The man from the West unfolded the little piece of paper handed him. His hand was steady when he began to read, but it trembled a little by the time he had finished. The note was rather short.

Bob: I was at the appointed place on time. When you struck the match to light your cigar I saw it was the face of the man wanted in Chicago. Somehow I couldn't do it myself, so I went around and got a plainclothesman to do the job.

JIMMY.

A Retrieved Reformation

A GUARD CAME to the prison shoe-shop, where Jimmy Valentine was assiduously stitching uppers, and escorted him to the front office. There the warden handed Jimmy his pardon, which had been signed that morning by the governor. Jimmy took it in a tired kind of way. He had served nearly ten months of a four year sentence. He had expected to stay only about three months, at the longest. When a man with as many friends on the outside as Jimmy Valentine had is received in the "stir"† it is hardly worth while to cut his hair.

"Now, Valentine," said the warden, "you'll go out in the morning. Brace up, and make a man of yourself. You're not a bad fellow at heart. Stop cracking safes, and live straight."

"Me?" said Jimmy, in surprise. "Why, I never cracked a safe in my life."

"Oh, no," laughed the warden. "Of course not. Let's see, now. How was it you happened to get sent up on that Springfield job? Was it because you wouldn't prove an alibi for fear of compromising somebody in extremely high-toned society? Or was it simply a case of a mean old jury that had it in for you? It's always one or the other with you innocent victims."

"Me?" said Jimmy, still blankly virtuous. "Why, warden, I never was in Springfield in my life!"

"Take him back, Cronin!" said the warden, "and fix him up with outgoing clothes. Unlock him at seven in the morning, and let him come to the bull-pen. Better think over my advice, Valentine."

At a quarter past seven on the next morning Jimmy stood in the warden's outer office. He had on a suit of the villainously fitting, ready-made clothes and a pair of the stiff, squeaky shoes that the state furnishes to its discharged compulsory guests.

The clerk handed him a railroad ticket and the five-dollar bill with which the law expected him to rehabilitate himself into good citizenship and prosperity. The warden gave him a cigar, and shook hands. Valentine, 9762, was chronicled on the books "Pardoned by Governor," and Mr. James Valentine walked out into the sunshine.

Disregarding the song of the birds, the waving green trees, and the smell of the flowers, Jimmy headed straight for a restaurant. There he tasted the first sweet joys of liberty in the shape of a broiled chicken and a bottle of white wine—followed by a cigar a grade better than the one the warden had given him. From there he proceeded leisurely to the depot. He tossed a quarter into the hat of a blind man sitting by the door, and boarded his train. Three hours set him down in a little town near the state line. He went to the cafe of one Mike Dolan and shook hands with Mike, who was alone behind the bar.

"Sorry we couldn't make it sooner, Jimmy, me boy," said Mike. "But we had that protest from Springfield to buck against, and the governor nearly balked. Feeling all right?"

"Fine," said Jimmy. "Got my key?"

He got his key and went upstairs, unlocking the door of a room at the rear. Everything was just as he had left it. There on the floor was still Ben Price's collar-button that had been torn from that eminent detective's shirt-band when they had overpowered Jimmy to arrest him.

Pulling out from the wall a folding-bed, Jimmy slid back a panel in the wall and dragged out a dust-covered suit-case. He opened this and gazed fondly at the finest set of burglar's tools in the East. It was a complete set, made of specially tempered steel, the latest designs in drills, punches, braces and bits, jimmies, clamps, and augers, with two or three novelties, invented by Jimmy himself, in which he took pride. Over nine hundred dollars they had cost him to have made at—, a place where they make such things for the profession.

In half an hour Jimmy went downstairs and through the cafe. He was now dressed in tasteful and well-fitting clothes, and carried his dusted and cleaned suit-case in his hand.

"Got anything on?" asked Mike Dolan, genially.

"Me?" said Jimmy, in a puzzled tone. "I don't understand. I'm representing the New York Amalgamated Short Snap Biscuit Cracker and Frazzled Wheat Company."

This statement delighted Mike to such an extent that Jimmy had to take a seltzer-and-milk on the spot. He never touched "hard" drinks.

A week after the release of Valentine, 9762, there was a neat job of safe-burglary done in Richmond, Indiana, with no clue to the author. A scant eight hundred dollars was all that was secured. Two weeks after that a patented, improved, burglar-proof safe in Logansport was opened like a cheese to the tune of fifteen hundred dollars, currency; securities and silver untouched. That began to interest the rogue-catchers. Then an old-fashioned bank-safe in Jefferson City became active and threw out of its crater an eruption of bank-notes amounting to five thousand dollars. The losses were now high enough to bring the matter up into Ben Price's class of work. By comparing notes, a remarkable similarity in the methods of the burglaries was noticed. Ben Price investigated the scenes of the robberies, and was heard to remark:

"That's Dandy Jim Valentine's autograph. He's resumed business. Look at that combination knob—jerked out as easy as pulling up a radish in wet weather. He's got the only clamps that can do it. And look how clean those tumblers were punched out! Jimmy never has to drill but one hole. Yes, I guess I want Mr. Valentine. He'll do his bit next time without any short-time or clemency foolishness."

Ben Price knew Jimmy's habits. He had learned them while working on the Springfield case. Long jumps, quick get-aways, no confederates, and a taste for good society—these ways had helped Mr. Valentine to become noted as a successful dodger of retribution. It was given out that Ben Price had taken up the trail of the elusive cracksman, and other people with burglar-proof safes felt more at ease.

One afternoon Jimmy Valentine and his suit-case climbed out of the mail-hack in Elmore, a little town five miles off the railroad down in the black-jack country of Arkansas. Jimmy, looking like an athletic young senior just home from college, went down the board side-walk toward the hotel.

A young lady crossed the street, passed him at the corner and entered a door over which was the sign "The Elmore Bank." Jimmy Valentine looked into her eyes, forgot what he was, and became another man. She lowered her eyes and colored slightly. Young men of Jimmy's style and looks were scarce in Elmore.

Jimmy collared a boy that was loafing on the steps of the bank as if he were one of the stockholders, and began to ask him questions about the town, feeding him dimes at intervals. By and by the young lady came out, looking royally unconscious of the young man with the suit-case, and went her way.

"Isn't that young lady Miss Polly Simpson?" asked Jimmy, with specious guile.

"Naw," said the boy. "She's Annabel Adams. Her pa owns this bank. What'd you come to Elmore for? Is that a gold watch-chain? I'm going to get a bulldog. Got any more dimes?"

Jimmy went to the Planters' Hotel, registered as Ralph D. Spencer, and engaged a room. He leaned on the desk and declared his platform to the clerk. He said he had come to Elmore to look for a location to go into business. How was the shoe business, now, in the town? He had thought of the shoe business. Was there an opening?

The clerk was impressed by the clothes and manner of Jimmy. He, himself, was something of a pattern of fashion to the thinly gilded youth of Elmore, but he now perceived his shortcomings. While trying to figure out Jimmy's manner of tying his four-in-hand he cordially gave information.

Yes, there ought to be a good opening in the shoe line. There wasn't an exclusive shoe-store in the place. The dry-goods and general stores handled them. Business in all lines was fairly good. Hoped Mr. Spencer would decide to locate in Elmore. He would find it a pleasant town to live in, and the people very sociable.

Mr. Spencer thought he would stop over in the town a few days and look over the situation. No, the clerk needn't call the boy. He would carry up his suit-case, himself; it was rather heavy.

Mr. Ralph Spencer, the phoenix that arose from Jimmy Valentine's ashes†—ashes left by the flame of a sudden and alterative attack of love—remained in Elmore, and prospered. He opened a shoe-store and secured a good run of trade.

Socially he was also a success, and made many friends. And he accomplished the wish of his heart. He met Miss Annabel Adams, and became more and more captivated by her charms.

At the end of a year the situation of Mr. Ralph Spencer was this: he had won the respect of the community, his shoe-store was flourishing, and he and Annabel were engaged to be married in two weeks. Mr. Adams, the typical, plodding, country banker, approved of Spencer. Annabel's pride in him almost equaled her affection. He was as much at home in the family of Mr.

Adams and that of Annabel's married sister as if he were already a member.

One day Jimmy sat down in his room and wrote this letter, which he mailed to the safe address of one of his old friends in St. Louis:

Dear Old Pal:

I want you to be at Sullivan's place, in Little Rock, next Wednesday night, at nine o'clock. I want you to wind up some little matters for me. And, also, I want to make you a present of my kit of tools. I know you'll be glad to get them—you couldn't duplicate the lot for a thousand dollars. Say, Billy, I've quit the old business—a year ago. I've got a nice store. I'm making an honest living, and I'm going to marry the finest girl on earth two weeks from now. It's the only life, Billy—the straight one. I wouldn't touch a dollar of another man's money now for a million. After I get married I'm going to sell out and go West, where there won't be so much danger of having old scores brought up against me. I tell you, Billy, she's an angel. She believes in me; and I wouldn't do another crooked thing for the whole world. Be sure to be at Sully's, for I must see you. I'll bring along the tools with me.

Your old friend,
Jimmy.

On the Monday night after Jimmy wrote this letter, Ben Price jogged unobtrusively into Elmore in a livery buggy. He lounged about town in his quiet way until he found out what he wanted to know. From the drug-store across the street from Spencer's shoe-store he got a good look at Ralph D. Spencer.

"Going to marry the banker's daughter are you, Jimmy?" said Ben to himself, softly. "Well, I don't know!"

The next morning Jimmy took breakfast at the Adamses. He was going to Little Rock that day to order his wedding-suit and buy something nice for Annabel. That would be the first time he had left town since he came to Elmore. It had been more than a year now since those last professional "jobs," and he thought he could safely venture out.

After breakfast quite a family party went downtown together—Mr. Adams, Annabel, Jimmy, and Annabel's married sister with her two little girls, aged five and nine. They came by the hotel where Jimmy still boarded, and he ran up to his room and brought along his suit-case. Then they went on to the bank. There stood Jimmy's horse and buggy and Dolph Gibson, who was going to drive him over to the railroad station.

All went inside the high, carved oak railings into the banking-room—Jimmy included, for Mr. Adams's future son-in-law was welcome anywhere. The clerks were pleased to be greeted by the good-looking, agreeable young man who was going to marry Miss Annabel. Jimmy set his suit-case down. Annabel, whose heart was bubbling with happiness and lively youth, put on Jimmy's hat, and picked up the suit-case. "Wouldn't I make a nice drummer?" said Annabel. "My! Ralph, how heavy it is. Feels like it was full of gold bricks."

"Lot of nickel-plated shoe-horns in there," said Jimmy, coolly, "that I'm going to return. Thought I'd save express charges by taking them up. I'm getting awfully economical."

The Elmore Bank had just put in a new safe and vault. Mr. Adams was very proud of it, and insisted on an inspection by every one. The vault was a small one, but it had a new, patented door. It fastened with three solid steel bolts thrown simultaneously with a single handle, and had a time-lock. Mr. Adams beamingly explained its workings to Mr. Spencer, who showed a courteous but not too intelligent interest. The two children, May and Agatha, were delighted by the shining metal and funny clock and knobs.

While they were thus engaged Ben Price sauntered in and leaned on his elbow, looking casually inside between the railings. He told the teller that he didn't want anything; he was just waiting for a man he knew.

Suddenly there was a scream or two from the women, and a commotion. Unperceived by the elders, May, the nine-year-old girl, in a spirit of play, had shut Agatha in the vault. She had then shot the bolts and turned the knob of the combination as she had seen Mr. Adams do.

The old banker sprang to the handle and tugged at it for a moment. "The door can't be opened," he groaned. "The clock hasn't been wound nor the combination set."

Agatha's mother screamed again, hysterically.

"Hush!" said Mr. Adams, raising his trembling hand. "All be quite for a moment. Agatha!" he called as loudly as he could. "Listen to me." During the following silence they could just hear the faint sound of the child wildly shrieking in the dark vault in a panic of terror.

"My precious darling!" wailed the mother. "She will die of fright! Open the door! Oh, break it open! Can't you men do something?"

"There isn't a man nearer than Little Rock who can open that door," said Mr. Adams, in a shaky voice. "My God! Spencer, what shall we do? That child—she can't stand it long in there. There isn't enough air, and, besides, she'll go into convulsions from fright."

Agatha's mother, frantic now, beat the door of the vault with her hands. Somebody wildly suggested dynamite. Annabel turned to Jimmy, her large eyes full of anguish, but not yet despairing. To a woman nothing seems quite impossible to the powers of the man she worships.

"Can't you do something, Ralph—*try*, won't you?"

He looked at her with a queer, soft smile on his lips and in his keen eyes.

"Annabel," he said, "give me that rose you are wearing, will you?"

Hardly believing that she heard him aright, she unpinned the bud from the bosom of her dress, and placed it in his hand. Jimmy stuffed it into his vest-pocket, threw off his coat and pulled up his shirt-sleeves. With that act Ralph D. Spencer passed away and Jimmy Valentine took his place.

"Get away from the door, all of you," he commanded, shortly.

He set his suit-case on the table, and opened it out flat. From that time on he seemed to be unconscious of the presence of any one else. He laid out the shining, queer implements swiftly and orderly, whistling softly to himself as he always did when at work. In a deep silence and immovable, the others watched him as if under a spell.

In a minute Jimmy's pet drill was biting smoothly into the steel door. In ten minutes—breaking his own burglarious record—he threw back the bolts and opened the door.

Agatha, almost collapsed, but safe, was gathered into her mother's arms.

Jimmy Valentine put on his coat, and walked outside the railings toward the front door. As he went he thought he heard a far-away voice that he once knew call "Ralph!" But he never hesitated.

At the door a big man stood somewhat in his way.

"Hello, Ben!" said Jimmy, still with his strange smile. "Got around at last, have you? Well, let's go. I don't know that it makes much difference, now."

And then Ben Price acted rather strangely.

"Guess you're mistaken, Mr. Spencer," he said. "Don't believe I recognize you. Your buggy's waiting for you, ain't it?"

And Ben Price turned and strolled down the street.

THE THIRD INGREDIENT

THE (SO-CALLED) VALLAMBROSA Apartment-House is not an apartment-house. It is composed of two old-fashioned, brownstone-front residences welded into one. The parlor floor of one side is gay with the wraps and head-gear of a modiste; the other is lugubrious with the sophistical promises and grisly display of a painless dentist. You may have a room there for two dollars a week or you may have one for twenty dollars. Among the Vallambrosa's roomers are stenographers, musicians, brokers, shop-girls, space-rate writers,† art students, wire-tappers, and other people who lean far over the banister-rail when the door-bell rings.

This treatise shall have to do with but two of the Vallambrosians—though meaning no disrespect to the others.

At six o'clock one afternoon Hetty Pepper came back to her third-floor rear $3.50 room in the Vallambrosa with her nose and chin more sharply pointed than usual. To be discharged from the department store where you have been working four years, and with only fifteen cents in your purse, does have a tendency to make your features appear more finely chiseled.

And now for Hetty's thumb-nail biography while she climbs the two flights of stairs.

She walked into the Biggest Store one morning four years before with seventy-five other girls, applying for a job behind the waist department counter. The phalanx of wage-earners formed a bewildering scene of beauty, carrying a total mass of blond hair sufficient to have justified the horseback gallops of a hundred Lady Godivas.†

The capable, cool-eyed, impersonal, young, bald-headed man whose task it was to engage six of the contestants, was aware of a feeling of suffocation as if he were drowning in a sea of frangipanni, while white clouds, hand-embroidered, floated about him. And then a sail hove in sight. Hetty Pepper, homely of countenance, with small, contemptuous, green eyes and chocolate-colored hair, dressed in a suit of plain burlap and a common-sense hat, stood before him with every one of her twenty-nine years of life unmistakably in sight.

"You're on!" shouted the bald-headed young man, and was saved. And that is how Hetty came to be employed in the Biggest Store. The story of her rise to an eight-dollar-a-week salary is the combined stories of Hercules,[†] Joan of Arc,[†] Una,[†] Job,[†] and Little-Red-Riding-Hood. You shall not learn from me the salary that was paid her as a beginner. There is a sentiment growing about such things, and I want no millionaire store-proprietors climbing the fire-escape of my tenement-house to throw dynamite bombs into my skylight boudoir.

The story of Hetty's discharge from the Biggest Store is so nearly a repetition of her engagement as to be monotonous.

In each department of the store there is an omniscient, omnipresent, and omnivorous person carrying always a mileage book and a red necktie, and referred to as a "buyer." The destinies of the girls in his department who live on (see Bureau of Victual Statistics)—so much per week are in his hands.

This particular buyer was a capable, cool-eyed, impersonal, young, bald-headed man. As he walked along the aisles of his department he seemed to be sailing on a sea of frangipanni, while white clouds, machine-embroidered, floated around him. Too many sweets bring surfeit. He looked upon Hetty Pepper's homely countenance, emerald eyes, and chocolate-colored hair as a welcome oasis of green in a desert of cloying beauty. In a quiet angle of a counter he pinched her arm kindly, three inches above the elbow. She slapped him three feet away with one good blow of her muscular and not especially lily-white right. So, now you know why Hetty Pepper came to leave the Biggest Store at thirty minutes' notice, with one dime and a nickel in her purse.

This morning's quotations list the price of rib beef at six cents per (butcher's) pound. But on the day that Hetty was "released" by the B. S. the price was seven and one-half cents. That fact is what makes this story possible. Otherwise, the extra four cents would have—

But the plot of nearly all the good stories in the world is concerned with shorts who were unable to cover; so you can find no fault with this one.

Hetty mounted with her rib beef to her $3.50 third-floor back. One hot, savory beef-stew for supper, a night's good sleep, and she would be fit in the morning to apply again for the tasks of Hercules, Joan of Arc, Una, Job, and Little-Red-Riding-Hood.

In her room she got the granite-ware stew-pan out of the 2x4-foot china—er—I mean earthenware closet, and began to dig down in a rat's-nest of paper bags for the potatoes and onions. She came out with her nose and chin just a little sharper pointed.

There was neither a potato nor an onion. Now, what kind of a beef-Stew can you make out of simply beef? You can make oyster-soup without oysters, turtle-soup without turtles, coffee-cake without coffee, but you can't make beef-stew without potatoes and onions.

But rib beef alone, in an emergency, can make an ordinary pine door look like a wrought-iron gambling-house portal to the wolf. With salt and pepper and a tablespoonful of flour (first well stirred in a little cold water) 'twill serve—'tis not so deep as a lobster à la Newburg nor so wide as a church festival doughnut; but 'twill serve.

Hetty took her stew-pan to the rear of the third-floor hall. According to the advertisements of the Vallambrosa there was running water to be found there. Between you and me and the water-meter, it only ambled or walked through the faucets; but technicalities have no place here. There was also a sink where housekeeping roomers often met to dump their coffee grounds and glare at one another's kimonos.

At this sink Hetty found a girl with heavy, gold-brown, artistic hair and plaintive eyes, washing two large "Irish" potatoes. Hetty knew the Vallambrosa as well as any one not owning "double hextra-magnifying eyes" could compass its mysteries. The kimonos were her encyclopedia, her "Who's What?" her clearinghouse of news, of goers and comers. From a rose-pink kimono edged with Nile green she had learned that the girl with the potatoes was a miniature-painter living in a kind of attic—or "studio," as they prefer to call it—on the top floor. Hetty was not certain in her mind what a miniature was; but it certainly wasn't a house; because house-painters, although they wear splashy overalls and poke ladders in your face on the street, are known to indulge in a riotous profusion of food at home.

The potato girl was quite slim and small, and handled her potatoes as an old bachelor uncle handles a baby who is cutting teeth. She had a dull shoemaker's knife in her right hand, and she had begun to peel one of the potatoes with it.

Hetty addressed her in the punctiliously formal tone of one who intends to be cheerfully familiar with you in the second round.

"Beg pardon," she said, "for butting into what's not my business, but if you peel them potatoes you lose out. They're new Bermudas. You want to scrape 'em. Lemme show you."

She took a potato and the knife, and began to demonstrate.

"Oh, thank you," breathed the artist. "I didn't know. And I did hate to see the thick peeling go; it seemed such a waste. But I thought they always had to be peeled. When you've got only potatoes to eat, the peelings count, you know."

"Say, kid," said Hetty, staying her knife, "you ain't up against it, too, are you?"

The miniature artist smiled starvedly.

"I suppose I am. Art—or, at least, the way I interpret it—doesn't seem to be much in demand. I have only these potatoes for my dinner. But they aren't so bad boiled and hot, with a little butter and salt."

"Child," said Hetty, letting a brief smile soften her rigid features, "Fate has sent me and you together. I've had it handed to me in the neck, too; but I've got a chunk of meat in my room as big as a lap-dog. And I've done everything to get potatoes except pray for 'em. Let's me and you bunch our commissary departments and make a stew of 'em. We'll cook it in my room. If we only had an onion to go in it! Say, kid, you haven't got a couple of pennies that've slipped down into the lining of your last winter's sealskin, have you? I could step down to the corner and get one at old Giuseppe's stand. A stew without an onion is worse'n a matinee without candy."

"You may call me Cecilia," said the artist. "No; I spent my last penny three days ago."

"Then we'll have to cut the onion out instead of slicing it in," said Hetty. "I'd ask the janitress for one, but I don't want 'em hep just yet to the fact that I'm pounding the asphalt for another job. But I wish we did have an onion."

In the shop-girl's room the two began to prepare their supper. Cecilia's part was to sit on the couch helplessly and beg to be allowed to do something, in the voice of a cooing ring-dove. Hetty prepared the rib beef, putting it in cold salted water in the stew-pan and setting it on the one-burner gas-stove.

"I wish we had an onion," said Hetty, as she scraped the two potatoes.

On the wall opposite the couch was pinned a flaming, gorgeous advertising picture of one of the new ferry-boats of the P. U. F. F. Railroad that had been built to cut down the time between Los Angeles and New York City one-eighth of a minute.

Hetty, turning her head during her continuous monologue, saw tears running from her guest's eyes as she gazed on the idealized presentment of the speeding, foam-girdled transport.

"Why, say, Cecilia, kid," said Hetty, poising her knife, "is it as bad art as that? I ain't a critic; but I thought it kind of brightened up the room. Of course, a manicure-painter could tell it was a bum picture in a minute. I'll take it down if you say so. I wish to the holy Saint Potluck we had an onion."

But the miniature miniature-painter had tumbled down, sobbing, with her nose indenting the hard-woven drapery of the couch. Something was here deeper than the artistic temperament offended at crude lithography.

Hetty knew. She had accepted her role long ago. How scant the words with which we try to describe a single quality of a human being! When we reach the abstract we are lost. The nearer to Nature that the babbling of our lips comes, the better do we understand. Figuratively (let us say), some people are Bosoms, some are Hands, some are Heads, some are Muscles, some are Feet, some are Backs for burdens.

Hetty was a Shoulder. Hers was a sharp, sinewy shoulder; but all her life people had laid their heads upon it, metaphorically or actually, and had left there all or half their troubles. Looking at Life anatomically, which is as good a way as any, she was preordained to be a Shoulder. There were few truer collar-bones anywhere than hers.

Hetty was only thirty-three, and she had not yet outlived the little pang that visited her whenever the head of youth and beauty leaned upon her for consolation. But one glance in her mirror always served as an instantaneous pain-killer. So she gave one pale look into the crinkly old looking-glass on the wall above the gas-stove, turned down the flame a little lower from the bubbling beef and potatoes, went over to the couch, and lifted Cecilia's head to its confessional.

"Go on and tell me, honey," she said. "I know now that it ain't art that's worrying you. You met him on a ferry-boat, didn't you? Go on, Cecilia, kid, and tell your—your Aunt Hetty about it."

But youth and melancholy must first spend the surplus of sighs and tears that waft and float the barque of romance to its harbor in the delectable isles. Presently, through the stringy tendons that formed the bars of the confessional, the penitent—or was it the glorified communicant of the sacred flame?—told her story without art or illumination.

"It was only three days ago. I was coming back on the ferry from Jersey City. Old Mr. Schrum, an art dealer, told me of a rich man in Newark who wanted a miniature of his daughter painted. I went to see him and showed him some of my work. When I told him the price would be fifty dollars he laughed at me like a hyena. He said an enlarged crayon twenty times the size would cost him only eight dollars.

"I had just enough money to buy my ferry ticket back to New York. I felt as if I didn't want to live another day. I must have looked as I felt, for I saw him on the row of seats opposite me, looking at me as if he understood. He was nice-looking, but oh, above everything else, he looked kind. When one is tired or unhappy or hopeless, kindness counts more than anything else.

"When I got so miserable that I couldn't fight against it any longer, I got up and walked slowly out the rear door of the ferry-boat cabin. No one was there, and I slipped quickly over the rail and dropped into the water. Oh, friend Hetty, it was cold, cold!

"For just one moment I wished I was back in the old Vallambrosa, starving and hoping. And then I got numb, and didn't care. And then I felt that somebody else was in the water close by me, holding me up. He had followed me, and jumped in to save me.

"Somebody threw a thing like a big, white doughnut at us, and he made me put my arms through the hole. Then the ferry-boat backed, and they pulled us on board. Oh, Hetty, I was so ashamed of my wickedness in trying to drown myself; and, besides, my hair had all tumbled down and was sopping wet, and I was such a sight.

"And then some men in blue clothes came around; and he gave them his card, and I heard him tell them he had seen me drop my purse on the edge of the boat outside the rail, and in leaning over to get it I had fallen overboard. And then I remembered having read in the papers that people who try to kill themselves are locked up in cells with people who try to kill other people, and I was afraid.

"But some ladies on the boat took me downstairs to the furnace-room and got me nearly dry and did up my hair. When the boat landed, he came and put me in a cab. He was all dripping himself, but laughed as if he thought it was all a joke. He begged me, but I wouldn't tell him my name nor where I lived, I was so ashamed."

"You were a fool, child," said Hetty, kindly. "Wait till I turn the light up a bit. I wish to Heaven we had an onion."

"Then he raised his hat," went on Cecilia, "and said: 'Very well. But I'll find you, anyhow. I'm going to claim my rights of salvage.' Then he gave money to the cab-driver and told him to take me where I wanted to go, and walked away. What is 'salvage,' Hetty?"

"The edge of a piece of goods that ain't hemmed," said the shop-girl. "You must have looked pretty well frazzled out to the little hero boy."

"It's been three days," moaned the miniature-painter, "and he hasn't found me yet."

"Extend the time," said Hetty. "This is a big town. Think of how many girls he might have to see soaked in water with their hair down before he would recognize you. The stew's getting on fine—but oh, for an onion! I'd even use a piece of garlic if I had it."

The beef and potatoes bubbled merrily, exhaling a mouth-watering savor that yet lacked something, leaving a hunger on the palate, a haunting, wistful desire for some lost and needful ingredient.

"I came near drowning in that awful river," said Cecilia, shuddering.

"It ought to have more water in it," said Hetty; "the stew, I mean. I'll go get some at the sink."

"It smells good," said the artist.

"That nasty old North River?" objected Hetty. "It smells to me like soap factories and wet setter-dogs—oh, you mean the stew. Well, I wish we had an onion for it. Did he look like he had money?"

"First, he looked kind," said Cecilia. "I'm sure he was rich; but that matters so little. When he drew out his bill-folder to pay the cab-man you couldn't help seeing hundreds and thousands of dollars in it. And I looked over the cab doors and saw him leave the ferry station in a motor-car; and the chauffeur gave him his bearskin to put on, for he was sopping wet. And it was only three days ago."

"What a fool!" said Hetty, shortly.

"Oh, the chauffeur wasn't wet," breathed Cecilia. "And he drove the car away very nicely."

"I mean you," said Hetty. "For not giving him your address."

"I never give my address to chauffeurs," said Cecilia, haughtily.

"I wish we had one," said Hetty, disconsolately.

"What for?"

"For the stew, of course—oh, I mean an onion."

Hetty took a pitcher and started to the sink at the end of the hall.

A young man came down the stairs from above just as she was opposite the lower step. He was decently dressed, but pale and haggard. His eyes were dull with the stress of some burden of physical or mental woe. In his hand he bore an onion—a pink, smooth, solid, shining onion as large around as a ninety-eight-cent alarm-clock.

Hetty stopped. So did the young man. There was something Joan of Arc-ish, Herculean, and Una-ish in the look and pose of the shoplady—she had cast off the roles of Job and Little-Red-Riding-Hood. The young man stopped at the foot of the stairs and coughed distractedly. He felt marooned, held up, attacked, assailed, levied upon, sacked, assessed, panhandled, browbeaten, though he knew not why. It was the look in Hetty's eyes that did it. In them he saw the Jolly Roger† fly to the masthead and an able seaman with a dirk between his teeth scurry up the ratlines and nail it there. But as yet he did not know that the cargo he carried was the thing that had caused him to be so nearly blown out of the water without even a parley.

"Beg your pardon," said Hetty, as sweetly as her dilute acetic acid tones permitted, "but did you find that onion on the stairs? There was a hole in the paper bag; and I've just come out to look for it."

The young man coughed for half a minute. The interval may have given him the courage to defend his own property. Also, he clutched his pungent prize greedily, and, with a show of spirit, faced his grim waylayer.

"No," he said huskily, "I didn't find it on the stairs. It was given to me by Jack Bevens, on the top floor. If you don't believe it, ask him. I'll wait until you do."

"I know about Bevens," said Hetty, sourly. "He writes books and things up there for the paper-and-rags man. We can hear the postman guy him all over the house when he brings them thick envelopes back. Say—do you live in the Vallambrosa?"

"I do not," said the young man. "I come to see Bevens sometimes. He's my friend. I live two blocks west."

"What are you going to do with the onion?—begging your pardon," said Hetty.

"I'm going to eat it."

"Raw?"

"Yes: as soon as I get home."

"Haven't you got anything else to eat with it?"

The young man considered briefly.

"No," he confessed; "there's not another scrap of anything in my diggings to eat. I think old Jack is pretty hard up for grub in his shack, too. He hated to give up the onion, but I worried him into parting with it."

"Man," said Hetty, fixing him with her world-sapient eyes, and laying a bony but impressive finger on his sleeve, "you've known trouble, too, haven't you?"

"Lots," said the onion owner, promptly. "But this onion is my own property, honestly come by. If you will excuse me, I must be going."

"Listen," said Hetty, paling a little with anxiety. "Raw onion is a mighty poor diet. And so is a beef-stew without one. Now, if you're Jack Bevens' friend, I guess you're nearly right. There's a little lady—a friend of mine—in my room there at the end of the hall. Both of us are out of luck; and we had just potatoes and meat between us. They're stewing now. But it ain't got any soul. There's something lacking to it. There's certain things in life that are naturally intended to fit and belong together. One is pink cheese-cloth and green roses, and one is ham and eggs, and one is Irish and trouble. And the other one is beef and potatoes with onions. And still another one is people who are up against it and other people in the same fix."

The young man went into a protracted paroxysm of coughing. With one hand he hugged his onion to his bosom.

"No doubt; no doubt," said he, at length. "But, as I said, I must be going, because—"

Hetty clutched his sleeve firmly.

"Don't be a Dago,† Little Brother. Don't eat raw onions. Chip it in toward the dinner and line yourself inside with the best stew you ever licked a spoon over. Must two ladies knock a young gentleman down and drag him inside for the honor of dining with 'em? No harm shall befall you, Little Brother. Loosen up and fall into line."

The young man's pale face relaxed into a grin.

"Believe I'll go you," he said, brightening. "If my onion is good as a credential, I'll accept the invitation gladly."

"It's good as that, but better as seasoning," said Hetty. "You come and stand outside the door till I ask my lady friend if she has any objections. And don't run away with that letter of recommendation before I come out."

Hetty went into her room and closed the door. The young man waited outside.

"Cecilia, kid," said the shop-girl, oiling the sharp saw of her voice as well as she could, "there's an onion outside. With a young man attached. I've asked him in to dinner. You ain't going to kick, are you?"

"Oh, dear!" said Cecilia, sitting up and patting her artistic hair. She cast a mournful glance at the ferry-boat poster on the wall.

"Nit," said Hetty. "It ain't him. You're up against real life now. I believe you said your hero friend had money and automobiles. This is a poor skeezicks† that's got nothing to eat but an onion. But he's easy-spoken and not a freshy. I imagine he's been a gentleman, he's so low down now. And we need the onion. Shall I bring him in? I'll guarantee his behavior."

"Hetty, dear," sighed Cecilia, "I'm so hungry. What difference does it make whether he's a prince or a burglar? I don't care. Bring him in if he's got anything to eat with him."

Hetty went back into the hall. The onion man was gone. Her heart missed a beat, and a gray look settled over her face except on her nose and cheek-bones. And then the tides of life flowed in again, for she saw him leaning out of the front window at the other end of the hall. She hurried there. He was shouting to some one below. The noise of the street overpowered the sound of her footsteps. She looked down over his shoulder, saw whom he was speaking to, and heard his words. He pulled himself in from the window-sill and saw her standing over him.

Hetty's eyes bored into him like two steel gimlets.

"Don't lie to me," she said, calmly. "What were you going to do with that onion?"

The young man suppressed a cough and faced her resolutely. His manner was that of one who had been bearded sufficiently.

"I was going to eat it," said he, with emphatic slowness; "just as I told you before."

"And you have nothing else to eat at home?"

"Not a thing."

"What kind of work do you do?"

"I am not working at anything just now."

"Then why," said Hetty, with her voice set on its sharpest edge, "do you lean out of windows and give orders to chauffeurs in green automobiles in the street below?"

The young man flushed, and his dull eyes began to sparkle.

"Because, madam," said he, in *accelerando*† tones, "I pay the chauffeur's wages and I own the automobile—and also this onion—this onion, madam."

He flourished the onion within an inch of Hetty's nose. The shop-lady did not retreat a hair's-breadth.

"Then why do you eat onions," she said, with biting contempt, "and nothing else?"

"I never said I did," retorted the young man, heatedly. "I said I had nothing else to eat where I live. I am not a delicatessen store-keeper."

"Then why," pursued Hetty, inflexibly, "were you going to eat a raw onion?"

"My mother," said the young man, "always made me eat one for a cold.

Pardon my referring to a physical infirmity; but you may have noticed that I have a very, very severe cold. I was going to eat the onion and go to bed. I wonder why I am standing here and apologizing to you for it."

"How did you catch this cold?" went on Hetty, suspiciously.

The young man seemed to have arrived at some extreme height of feeling. There were two modes of descent open to him—a burst of rage or a surrender to the ridiculous. He chose wisely; and the empty hall echoed his hoarse laughter.

"You're a dandy," said he. "And I don't blame you for being careful. I don't mind telling you. I got wet. I was on a North River ferry a few days ago when a girl jumped overboard. Of course, I—"

Hetty extended her hand, interrupting his story.

"Give me the onion," she said.

The young man set his jaw a trifle harder.

"Give me the onion," she repeated.

He grinned, and laid it in her hand.

Then Hetty's infrequent, grim, melancholy smile showed itself. She took the young man's arm and pointed with her other hand to the door of her room.

"Little Brother," she said, "go in there. The little fool you fished out of the river is there waiting for you. Go on in. I'll give you three minutes before I come. Potatoes is in there, waiting. Go on in, Onions."

After he had tapped at the door and entered, Hetty began to peel and wash the onion at the sink. She gave a gray look at the gray roofs outside, and the smile on her face vanished by little jerks and twitches.

"But it's us," she said, grimly, to herself, "it's us that furnishes the beef."

The Princess and the Puma†

THERE HAD TO be a king and queen, of course. The king was a terrible old man who wore six-shooters and spurs, and shouted in such a tremendous voice that the rattlers on the prairie would run into their holes under the prickly pear. Before there was a royal family they called the man "Whispering Ben." When he came to own 50,000 acres of land and more cattle than he could count, they called him O'Donnell "the Cattle King."

The queen had been a Mexican girl from Laredo.† She made a good, mild, Colorado-claro† wife, and even succeeded in teaching Ben to modify his voice sufficiently while in the house to keep the dishes from being broken. When Ben got to be king she would sit on the gallery of Espinosa Ranch and weave rush mats. When wealth became so irresistible and oppressive that upholstered chairs and a centre table were brought down from San Antone in the wagons, she bowed her smooth, dark head, and shared the fate of the Danaë.†

To avoid *lèse-majeste*† you have been presented first to the king and queen. They do not enter the story, which might be called "The Chronicle of the Princess, the Happy Thought, and the Lion that Bungled his Job."

Josefa O'Donnell was the surviving daughter, the princess. From her mother she inherited warmth of nature and a dusky, semi-tropic beauty. From Ben O'Donnell the royal she acquired a store of intrepidity, common sense, and the faculty of ruling. The combination was one worth going miles to see. Josefa while riding her pony at a gallop could put five out of six bullets through a tomato-can swinging at the end of a string. She could play for hours with a white kitten she owned, dressing it in all manner of absurd clothes. Scorning a pencil, she could tell you out of her head what 1545 two-year-olds would bring on the hoof, at $8.50 per head. Roughly speaking, the Espinosa Ranch is forty miles long and thirty broad—but mostly leased land. Josefa, on her pony, had prospected over every mile of it. Every cow-puncher on the range knew her by sight and was a loyal vassal. Ripley Givens, foreman of one of the Espinosa outfits, saw her one day, and made up his mind to form a royal matrimonial alliance. Presumptuous? No. In those days in the Nueces country† a man was a man. And, after all, the title of cattle king does not presuppose blood royalty. Often it only signifies that its owner wears the crown in token of his magnificent qualities in the art of cattle stealing.

One day Ripley Givens rode over to the Double Elm Ranch to inquire about a bunch of strayed yearlings. He was late in setting out on his return trip, and it was sundown when he struck the White Horse Crossing of the Nueces. From there to his own camp it was sixteen miles. To the Espinosa ranch it was twelve. Givens was tired. He decided to pass the night at the Crossing.

There was a fine water hole in the river-bed. The banks were thickly covered with great trees, undergrown with brush. Back from the water hole fifty yards was a stretch of curly mesquite grass—supper for his horse and bed for himself. Givens staked his horse, and spread out his saddle blankets to dry. He sat down with his back against a tree and rolled a cigarette. From somewhere in the dense timber along the river came a sudden, rageful, shivering wail. The pony danced at the end of his rope and blew a whistling snort of comprehending fear. Givens puffed at his cigarette, but he reached leisurely for his pistol-belt, which lay on the grass, and twirled the cylinder of his weapon tentatively. A great gar plunged with a loud splash into the water hole. A little brown rabbit skipped around a bunch of catclaw and sat twitching his whiskers and looking humorously at Givens. The pony went on eating grass.

It is well to be reasonably watchful when a Mexican lion† sings soprano along the arroyos at sundown. The burden of his song may be that young calves and fat lambs are scarce, and that he has a carnivorous desire for your acquaintance.

In the grass lay an empty fruit can, cast there by some former sojourner. Givens caught sight of it with a grunt of satisfaction. In his coat pocket tied behind his saddle was a handful or two of ground coffee. Black coffee and cigarettes! What ranchero could desire more?

In two minutes he had a little fire going clearly. He started, with his can, for the water hole. When within fifteen yards of its edge he saw, between the bushes, a side-saddled pony with down-dropped reins cropping grass a little distance to his left. Just rising from her hands and knees on the brink of the water hole was Josefa O'Donnell. She had been drinking water, and she brushed the sand from the palms of her hands. Ten yards away, to her right, half concealed by a clump of sacuista, Givens saw the crouching form of the Mexican lion. His amber eyeballs glared hungrily; six feet from them was the tip of the tail stretched straight, like a pointer's. His hind-quarters rocked with the motion of the cat tribe preliminary to leaping.

Givens did what he could. His six-shooter was thirty-five yards away lying on the grass. He gave a loud yell, and dashed between the lion and the princess.

The "rucus," as Givens called it afterward, was brief and somewhat confused. When he arrived on the line of attack he saw a dim streak in the air, and heard a couple of faint cracks. Then a hundred pounds of Mexican lion plumped down upon his head and flattened him, with a heavy jar, to the ground. He remembered calling out: "Let up, now—no fair gouging!" and then he crawled from under the lion like a worm, with his mouth full of grass and dirt, and a big lump on the back of his head where it had struck the root of a water-elm. The lion lay motionless. Givens, feeling aggrieved, and suspicious of fouls, shook his fist at the lion, and shouted: "I'll rastle you again for twenty—" and then he got back to himself.

Josefa was standing in her tracks, quietly reloading her silver-mounted .38. It had not been a difficult shot. The lion's head made an easier mark than a tomato-can swinging at the end of a string. There was a provoking, teasing, maddening smile upon her mouth and in her dark eyes. The would-be-rescuing knight felt the fire of his fiasco burn down to his soul. Here had been his chance, the chance that he had dreamed of; and Momus,[†] and not Cupid,[†] had presided over it. The satyrs in the wood were, no doubt, holding their sides in hilarious, silent laughter. There had been something like vaudeville—say Signor Givens and his funny knockabout act with the stuffed lion.

"Is that you, Mr. Givens?" said Josefa, in her deliberate, saccharine contralto. "You nearly spoilt my shot when you yelled. Did you hurt your head when you fell?"

"Oh, no," said Givens, quietly; "that didn't hurt." He stooped ignominiously and dragged his best Stetson hat from under the beast. It was crushed and wrinkled to a fine comedy effect. Then he knelt down and softly stroked the fierce, open-jawed head of the dead lion.

"Poor old Bill!" he exclaimed mournfully.

"What's that?" asked Josefa, sharply.

"Of course you didn't know, Miss Josefa," said Givens, with an air of one allowing magnanimity to triumph over grief. "Nobody can blame you. I tried to save him, but I couldn't let you know in time."

"Save who?"

"Why, Bill. I've been looking for him all day. You see, he's been our camp pet for two years. Poor old fellow, he wouldn't have hurt a cottontail rabbit. It'll break the boys all up when they hear about it. But you couldn't tell, of course, that Bill was just trying to play with you."

Josefa's black eyes burned steadily upon him. Ripley Givens met the test successfully. He stood rumpling the yellow-brown curls on his head pensively. In his eye was regret, not unmingled with a gentle reproach. His smooth features were set to a pattern of indisputable sorrow. Josefa wavered.

"What was your pet doing here?" she asked, making a last stand. "There's no camp near the White Horse Crossing."

"The old rascal ran away from camp yesterday," answered Givens readily. "It's a wonder the coyotes didn't scare him to death. You see, Jim Webster, our horse wrangler, brought a little terrier pup into camp last week. The pup made life miserable for Bill—he used to chase him around and chew his hind legs for hours at a time. Every night when bedtime came Bill would sneak under one of the boy's blankets and sleep to keep the pup from finding him. I reckon he must have been worried pretty desperate or he wouldn't have run away. He was always afraid to get out of sight of camp."

Josefa looked at the body of the fierce animal. Givens gently patted one of the formidable paws that could have killed a yearling calf with one blow. Slowly a red flush widened upon the dark olive face of the girl. Was it the signal of shame of the true sportsman who has brought down ignoble quarry? Her eyes grew softer, and the lowered lids drove away all their bright mockery.

"I'm very sorry," she said humbly; "but he looked so big, and jumped so high that—"

"Poor old Bill was hungry," interrupted Givens, in quick defence of the deceased. "We always made him jump for his supper in camp. He would lie down and roll over for a piece of meat. When he saw you he thought he was going to get something to eat from you."

Suddenly Josefa's eyes opened wide.

"I might have shot you!" she exclaimed. "You ran right in between. You risked your life to save your pet! That was fine, Mr. Givens. I like a man who is kind to animals."

Yes; there was even admiration in her gaze now. After all, there was a hero rising out of the ruins of the anti-climax. The look on Givens's face would have secured him a high position in the S.P.C.A.[†]

"I always loved 'em," said he; "horses, dogs, Mexican lions, cows, alligators—"

"I hate alligators," instantly demurred Josefa; "crawly, muddy things!"

"Did I say alligators?" said Givens. "I meant antelopes, of course."

Josefa's conscience drove her to make further amends. She held out her hand penitently. There was a bright, unshed drop in each of her eyes.

"Please forgive me, Mr. Givens, won't you? I'm only a girl, you know, and I was frightened at first. I'm very, very sorry I shot Bill. You don't know how ashamed I feel. I wouldn't have done it for anything."

Givens took the proffered hand. He held it for a time while he allowed the generosity of his nature to overcome his grief at the loss of Bill. At last it was clear that he had forgiven her.

"Please don't speak of it any more, Miss Josefa. 'Twas enough to frighten any young lady the way Bill looked. I'll explain it all right to the boys."

"Are you really sure you don't hate me?" Josefa came closer to him impulsively. Her eyes were sweet—oh, sweet and pleading with gracious penitence. "I would hate anyone who would kill my kitten. And how daring and kind of you to risk being shot when you tried to save him! How very few men would have done that!" Victory wrested from defeat! Vaudeville turned into drama! Bravo, Ripley Givens!

It was now twilight. Of course Miss Josefa could not be allowed to ride on to the ranch-house alone. Givens resaddled his pony in spite of that animal's reproachful glances, and rode with her. Side by side they galloped across the smooth grass, the princess and the man who was kind to animals. The prairie odors of fruitful earth and delicate bloom were thick and sweet around them. Coyotes yelping over there on the hill! No fear. And yet—Josefa rode closer. A little hand seemed to grope. Givens found it with his own. The ponies kept an even gait. The hands lingered together, and the owner of one explained:

"I never was frightened before, but just think! How terrible it would be to meet a really wild lion! Poor Bill! I'm so glad you came with me!"

O'Donnell was sitting on the ranch gallery.

"Hello, Rip!" he shouted—"that you?"

"He rode in with me," said Josefa. "I lost my way and was late."

"Much obliged," called the cattle king. "Stop over, Rip, and ride to camp in the morning."

But Givens would not. He would push on to camp. There was a bunch of steers to start off on the trail at daybreak. He said good-night, and trotted away.

An hour later, when the lights were out, Josefa, in her night-robe, came to her door and called to the king in his own room across the brick-paved hallway:

"Say, pop, you know that old Mexican lion they call the 'Gotch-eared Devil'—the one that killed Gonzales, Mr. Martin's sheep herder, and about fifty calves on the Salado range? Well, I settled his hash this afternoon over at the White Horse Crossing. Put two balls in his head with my .38 while he was on the jump. I knew him by the slice gone from his left ear that old Gonzales cut off with his machete. You couldn't have made a better shot yourself, daddy."

"Bully for you!" thundered Whispering Ben from the darkness of the royal chamber.

Buried Treasure

THERE ARE MANY kinds of fools. Now, will everybody please sit still until they are called upon specifically to rise?

I had been every kind of fool except one. I had expended my patrimony, pretended my matrimony, played poker, lawn-tennis, and bucket-shops†—parted soon with my money in many ways. But there remained one rule of the wearer of cap and bells that I had not played. That was the Seeker after Buried Treasure. To few does the delectable furor come. But of all the would-be followers in the hoof-prints of King Midas† none has found a pursuit so rich in pleasurable promise.

But, going back from my theme a while—as lame pens must do—I was a fool of the sentimental sort. I saw May Martha Mangum, and was hers. She was eighteen, the color of the white ivory keys of a new piano, beautiful, and possessed by the exquisite solemnity and pathetic witchery of an unsophisticated angel doomed to live in a small, dull, Texas prairie-town. She had a spirit and charm that could have enabled her to pluck rubies like raspberries from the crown of Belgium or any other sporty kingdom, but she did not know it, and I did not paint the picture for her.

You see, I wanted May Martha Mangum for to have and to hold.† I wanted her to abide with me, and put my slippers and pipe away every day in places where they cannot be found of evenings.

May Martha's father was a man hidden behind whiskers and spectacles. He lived for bugs and butterflies and all insects that fly or crawl or buzz or get down your back or in the butter. He was an etymologist, or words to that effect.† He spent his life seining the air for flying fish of the June-bug order, and then sticking pins through 'em and calling 'em names.

He and May Martha were the whole family. He prized her highly as a fine specimen of the racibus humanus† because she saw that he had food at times, and put his clothes on right side before, and kept his alcohol-bottles filled. Scientists, they say, are apt to be absent-minded.

There was another besides myself who thought May Martha Mangum one to be desired. That was Goodloe Banks, a young man just home from college. He had all the attainments to be found in books—Latin, Greek, philosophy, and especially the higher branches of mathematics and logic.

If it hadn't been for his habit of pouring out this information and learning on every one that he addressed, I'd have liked him pretty well. But, even as it was, he and I were, you would have thought, great pals.

We got together every time we could because each of us wanted to pump the other for whatever straws we could to find which way the wind blew from the heart of May Martha Mangum—rather a mixed metaphor; Goodloe Banks would never have been guilty of that. That is the way of rivals.

You might say that Goodloe ran to books, manners, culture, rowing, intellect, and clothes. I would have put you in mind more of baseball and Friday-night debating societies—by way of culture—and maybe of a good horseback rider.

But in our talks together, and in our visits and conversation with May Martha, neither Goodloe Banks nor I could find out which one of us she preferred. May Martha was a natural-born non-committal, and knew in her cradle how to keep people guessing.

As I said, old man Mangum was absentminded. After a long time he found out one day—a little butterfly must have told him—that two young men were trying to throw a net over the head of the young person, a daughter, or some such technical appendage, who looked after his comforts.

I never knew scientists could rise to such occasions. Old Mangum orally labelled and classified Goodloe and myself easily among the lowest orders of the vertebrates; and in English, too, without going any further into Latin than the simple references to Orgetorix, Rex Helvetii†—which is as far as I ever went, myself. And he told us that if he ever caught us around his house again he would add us to his collection.

Goodloe Banks and I remained away five days, expecting the storm to subside. When we dared to call at the house again May Martha Mangum and her father were gone. Gone! The house they had rented was closed. Their little store of goods and chattels was gone also.

And not a word of farewell to either of us from May Martha—not a white, fluttering note pinned to the hawthorn-bush; not a chalk-mark on the gate-post nor a post-card in the post-office to give us a clew.

For two months Goodloe Banks and I—separately—tried every scheme we could think of to track the runaways. We used our friendship and influence with the ticket-agent, with livery-stable men, railroad conductors, and our one lone, lorn constable, but without results.

Then we became better friends and worse enemies than ever. We forgathered in the back room of Snyder's saloon every afternoon after work, and played dominoes, and laid conversational traps to find out from each other if anything had been discovered. That is the way of rivals.

Now, Goodloe Banks had a sarcastic way of displaying his own learning and putting me in the class that was reading "Poor Jane Ray, her bird is dead, she cannot play." Well, I rather liked Goodloe, and I had a contempt for his college learning, and I was always regarded as good-natured, so I kept my temper. And I was trying to find out if he knew anything about May Martha, so I endured his society.

In talking things over one afternoon he said to me:

"Suppose you do find her, Ed, whereby would you profit? Miss Mangum has a mind. Perhaps it is yet uncultured, but she is destined for higher things than you could give her. I have talked with no one who seemed to appreciate more the enchantment of the ancient poets and writers and the modern cults that have assimilated and expended their philosophy of life. Don't you think you are wasting your time looking for her?"

"My idea," said I, "of a happy home is an eight-room house in a grove of live-oaks by the side of a charco† on a Texas prairie. A piano," I went on, "with an automatic player in the sitting-room, three thousand head of cattle under fence for a starter, a buckboard and ponies always hitched at a post for 'the missus'—and May Martha Mangum to spend the profits of the ranch as she pleases, and to abide with me, and put my slippers and pipe away every day in places where they cannot be found of evenings. That," said I, "is what is to be; and a fig—a dried, Smyrna, dago-stand fig†—for your curriculums, cults, and philosophy."

"She is meant for higher things," repeated Goodloe Banks.

"Whatever she is meant for," I answered, just now she is out of pocket. And I shall find her as soon as I can without aid of the colleges."

"The game is blocked," said Goodloe, putting down a domino; and we had the beer.

Shortly after that a young farmer whom I knew came into town and brought me a folded blue paper. He said his grandfather had just died. I concealed a tear, and he went on to say that the old man had jealously guarded this paper for twenty years. He left it to his family as part of his estate, the rest of which consisted of two mules and a hypotenuse of non-arable land.

The sheet of paper was of the old, blue kind used during the rebellion of the abolitionists against the secessionists.† It was dated June 14, 1863, and it described the hiding-place of ten burro-loads of gold and silver coin valued at three hundred thousand dollars. Old Rundle—grandfather of his grandson, Sam—was given the information by a Spanish priest who was in on the treasure-burying, and who died many years before—no, afterward—in old Rundle's house. Old Rundle wrote it down from dictation.

"Why didn't your father look this up?" I asked young Rundle.

"He went blind before he could do so," he replied.

"Why didn't you hunt for it yourself?" I asked.

"Well," said he, "I've only known about the paper for ten years. First there was the spring ploughin' to do, and then choppin' the weeds out of the corn; and then come takin' fodder; and mighty soon winter was on us. It seemed to run along that way year after year."

That sounded perfectly reasonable to me, so I took it up with young Lee Rundle at once.

The directions on the paper were simple. The whole burro cavalcade laden with the treasure started from an old Spanish mission in Dolores County. They travelled due south by the compass until they reached the Alamito River. They forded this, and buried the treasure on the top of a little mountain shaped like a pack-saddle standing in a row between two higher ones. A heap of stones marked the place of the buried treasure. All the party except the Spanish priest were killed by Indians a few days later. The secret was a monopoly. It looked good to me.

Lee Rundle suggested that we rig out a camping outfit, hire a surveyor to run out the line from the Spanish mission, and then spend the three hundred thousand dollars seeing the sights in Fort Worth.† But, without being highly educated, I knew a way to save time and expense.

We went to the State land-office and had a practical, what they call a "working," sketch made of all the surveys of land from the old mission to the Alamito River. On this map I drew a line due southward to the river. The length of lines of each survey and section of land was accurately given on the sketch. By these we found the point on the river and had a "connection" made with it and an important, well-identified corner of the Los Animos five-league survey—a grant made by King Philip of Spain.†

By doing this we did not need to have the line run out by a surveyor. It was a great saving of expense and time.

So, Lee Rundle and I fitted out a two-horse wagon team with all the accessories, and drove a hundred and forty-nine miles to Chico, the nearest town to the point we wished to reach. There we picked up a deputy county surveyor. He found the corner of the Los Animos survey for us, ran out the five thousand seven hundred and twenty varas west that our sketch called for, laid a stone on the spot, had coffee and bacon, and caught the mail-stage back to Chico.

I was pretty sure we would get that three hundred thousand dollars. Lee Rundle's was to be only one-third, because I was paying all the expenses. With that two hundred thousand dollars I knew I could find May Martha Mangum if she was on earth. And with it I could flutter the butterflies in old man Mangum's dove-cot, too. If I could find that treasure!

But Lee and I established camp. Across the river were a dozen little mountains densely covered by cedar-brakes, but not one shaped like a pack-saddle. That did not deter us. Appearances are deceptive. A pack-saddle, like beauty, may exist only in the eye of the beholder.

I and the grandson of the treasure examined those cedar-covered hills with the care of a lady hunting for the wicked flea. We explored every side, top, circumference, mean elevation, angle, slope, and concavity of every one for two miles up and down the river. We spent four days doing so. Then we hitched up the roan and the dun,† and hauled the remains of the coffee and bacon the one hundred and forty-nine miles back to Concho City.

Lee Rundle chewed much tobacco on the return trip. I was busy driving, because I was in a hurry.

As shortly as could be after our empty return Goodloe Banks and I forgathered in the back room of Snyder's saloon to play dominoes and fish for information. I told Goodloe about my expedition after the buried treasure.

"If I could have found that three hundred thousand dollars," I said to him, "I could have scoured and sifted the surface of the earth to find May Martha Mangum."

"She is meant for higher things," said Goodloe. "I shall find her myself. But, tell me how you went about discovering the spot where this unearthed increment was imprudently buried."

I told him in the smallest detail. I showed him the draughtsman's sketch with the distances marked plainly upon it.

After glancing over it in a masterly way, he leaned back in his chair and bestowed upon me an explosion of sardonic, superior, collegiate laughter.

"Well, you are a fool, Jim," he said, when he could speak.

"It's your play," said I, patiently, fingering my double-six.

"Twenty," said Goodloe, making two crosses on the table with his chalk.

"Why am I a fool?" I asked. "Buried treasure has been found before in many places."

"Because," said he, "in calculating the point on the river where your line would strike you neglected to allow for the variation. The variation there would be nine degrees west. Let me have your pencil."

Goodloe Banks figured rapidly on the back of an envelope.

"The distance, from north to south, of the line run from the Spanish mission," said he, "is exactly twenty-two miles. It was run by a pocket-compass, according to your story. Allowing for the variation, the point on the Alamito River where you should have searched for your treasure is exactly six miles and nine hundred and forty-five varas farther west than the place you hit upon. Oh, what a fool you are, Jim!"

"What is this variation that you speak of?" I asked. "I thought figures never lied."

"The variation of the magnetic compass," said Goodloe, "from the true meridian."†

He smiled in his superior way; and then I saw come out in his face the singular, eager, consuming cupidity of the seeker after buried treasure.

"Sometimes," he said with the air of the oracle, "these old traditions of hidden money are not without foundation. Suppose you let me look over that paper describing the location. Perhaps together we might—"

The result was that Goodloe Banks and I, rivals in love, became companions in adventure. We went to Chico by stage from Huntersburg, the nearest railroad town. In Chico we hired a team drawing a covered spring-wagon and camping paraphernalia. We had the same surveyor run out our distance, as revised by Goodloe and his variations, and then dismissed him and sent him on his homeward road.

It was night when we arrived. I fed the horses and made a fire near the bank of the river and cooked supper. Goodloe would have helped, but his education had not fitted him for practical things.

But while I worked he cheered me with the expression of great thoughts handed down from the dead ones of old. He quoted some translations from the Greek at much length.

"Anacreon,"† he explained. "That was a favorite passage with Miss Mangum—as I recited it."

"She is meant for higher things," said I, repeating his phrase.

"Can there be anything higher," asked Goodloe, "than to dwell in the society of the classics, to live in the atmosphere of learning and culture? You have often decried education. What of your wasted efforts through your ignorance of simple mathematics? How soon would you have found your treasure if my knowledge had not shown you your error?"

"We'll take a look at those hills across the river first," said I, "and see what we find. I am still doubtful about variations. I have been brought up to believe that the needle is true to the pole."

The next morning was a bright June one. We were up early and had breakfast. Goodloe was charmed. He recited—Keats, I think it was, and Kelly or Shelley†—while I broiled the bacon. We were getting ready to cross the river, which was little more than a shallow creek there, and explore the many sharp-peaked cedar-covered hills on the other side.

"My good Ulysses,"† said Goodloe, slapping me on the shoulder while I was washing the tin breakfast-plates, "let me see the enchanted document once more. I believe it gives directions for climbing the hill shaped like a pack-saddle. I never saw a pack-saddle. What is it like, Jim?"

"Score one against culture," said I. "I'll know it when I see it."

Goodloe was looking at old Rundle's document when he ripped out a most uncollegiate swear-word.

"Come here," he said, holding the paper up against the sunlight. "Look at that," he said, laying his finger against it.

On the blue paper—a thing I had never noticed before—I saw stand out in white letters the word and figures: "Malvern, 1898."

"What about it?" I asked.

"It's the water-mark," said Goodloe. "The paper was manufactured in 1898. The writing on the paper is dated 1863. This is a palpable fraud."

"Oh, I don't know," said I. "The Rundles are pretty reliable, plain, uneducated country people. Maybe the paper manufacturers tried to perpetrate a swindle."

And then Goodloe Banks went as wild as his education permitted. He dropped the glasses off his nose and glared at me.

"I've often told you you were a fool," he said. "You have let yourself be imposed upon by a clodhopper. And you have imposed upon me."

"How," I asked, "have I imposed upon you?"

"By your ignorance," said he. "Twice I have discovered serious flaws in your plans that a common-school education should have enabled you to avoid. And," he continued, "I have been put to expense that I could ill afford in pursuing this swindling quest. I am done with it."

I rose and pointed a large pewter spoon at him, fresh from the dish-water.

"Goodloe Banks," I said, "I care not one parboiled navy bean for your education. I always barely tolerated it in any one, and I despised it in you. What has your learning done for you? It is a curse to yourself and a bore to your friends. Away," I said—"away with your water-marks and variations! They are nothing to me. They shall not deflect me from the quest."

I pointed with my spoon across the river to a small mountain shaped like a pack-saddle.

"I am going to search that mountain," I went on, "for the treasure. Decide now whether you are in it or not. If you wish to let a water-mark or a variation shake your soul, you are no true adventurer. Decide."

A white cloud of dust began to rise far down the river road. It was the mail-wagon from Hesperus to Chico. Goodloe flagged it.

"I am done with the swindle," said he, sourly. "No one but a fool would pay any attention to that paper now. Well, you always were a fool, Jim. I leave you to your fate."

He gathered his personal traps, climbed into the mail-wagon, adjusted his glasses nervously, and flew away in a cloud of dust.

After I had washed the dishes and staked the horses on new grass, I crossed the shallow river and made my way slowly through the cedar-brakes up to the top of the hill shaped like a pack-saddle.

It was a wonderful June day. Never in my life had I seen so many birds, so many butter-flies, dragon-flies, grasshoppers, and such winged and stinged beasts of the air and fields.

I investigated the hill shaped like a pack-saddle from base to summit. I found an absolute absence of signs relating to buried treasure. There was no pile of stones, no ancient blazes on the trees, none of the evidences of the three hundred thousand dollars, as set forth in the document of old man Rundle.

I came down the hill in the cool of the afternoon. Suddenly, out of the cedar-brake I stepped into a beautiful green valley where a tributary small stream ran into the Alamito River.

And there I was startled to see what I took to be a wild man, with unkempt beard and ragged hair, pursuing a giant butterfly with brilliant wings.

"Perhaps he is an escaped madman," I thought; and wondered how he had strayed so far from seats of education and learning.

And then I took a few more steps and saw a vine-covered cottage near the small stream. And in a little grassy glade I saw May Martha Mangum plucking wild flowers.

She straightened up and looked at me. For the first time since I knew her I saw her face—which was the color of the white keys of a new piano—turn pink. I walked toward her without a word. She let the gathered flowers trickle slowly from her hand to the grass.

"I knew you would come, Jim," she said clearly. "Father wouldn't let me write, but I knew you would come.

What followed you may guess—there was my wagon and team just across the river.

I've often wondered what good too much education is to a man if he can't use it for himself. If all the benefits of it are to go to others, where does it come in?

For May Martha Mangum abides with me. There is an eight-room house in a live-oak grove, and a piano with an automatic player, and a good start toward the three thousand head of cattle is under fence.

And when I ride home at night my pipe and slippers are put away in places where they cannot be found.

But who cares for that? Who cares—who cares?

An Unfinished Story

We no longer groan and heap ashes upon our heads when the flames of Tophet† are mentioned. For, even the preachers have begun to tell us that God is radium, or ether or some scientific compound, and that the worst we wicked ones may expect is a chemical reaction. This is a pleasing hypothesis; but there lingers yet some of the old, goodly terror of orthodoxy.

There are but two subjects upon which one may discourse with a free imagination, and without the possibility of being controverted. You may talk of your dreams; and you may tell what you heard a parrot say. Both Morpheus† and the bird are incompetent witnesses; and your listener dare not attack your recital. The baseless fabric of a vision, then, shall furnish my theme—chosen with apologies and regrets instead of the more limited field of Pretty Polly's small talk.

I had a dream that was so far removed from the higher criticism that it had to do with the ancient, respectable, and lamented bar-of-judgment theory.

Gabriel had played his trump;† and those of us who could not follow suit were arraigned for examination. I noticed at one side a gathering of professional bondsmen in solemn black and collars that buttoned behind; but it seemed there was some trouble about their real estate titles; and they did not appear to be getting any of us out.

A fly cop—an angel policeman—flew over to me and took me by the left wing. Near at hand was a group of very prosperous-looking spirits arraigned for judgment.

"Do you belong with that bunch?" the policeman asked.

"Who are they?" was my answer.

"Why," said he, "they are—"

But this irrelevant stuff is taking up space that the story should occupy.

Dulcie worked in a department store. She sold Hamburg edging,† or stuffed peppers, or automobiles, or other little trinkets such as they keep in department stores. Of what she earned, Dulcie received six dollars per week. The remainder was credited to her and debited to somebody else's account in the ledger kept by G—Oh, primal energy, you say, Reverend Doctor—Well then, in the Ledger of Primal Energy.

During her first year in the store, Dulcie was paid five dollars per week. It would be instructive to know how she lived on that amount. Don't care? Very well; probably you are interested in larger amounts. Six dollars is a larger amount. I will tell you how she lived on six dollars per week.

One afternoon at six, when Dulcie was sticking her hat-pin within an eighth of an inch of her medulla oblongata, she said to her chum, Sadie—the girl that waits on you with her left side:

"Say, Sade, I made a date for dinner this evening with Piggy."

"You never did!" exclaimed Sadie admiringly. "Well, ain't you the lucky one? Piggy's an awful swell; and he always takes a girl to swell places. He took Blanche up to the Hoffman House one evening, where they have swell music, and you see a lot of swells. You'll have a swell time, Dulcie."

Dulcie hurried off homeward. Her eyes were shining, and her cheeks showed the delicate pink of life's—real life's—approaching dawn. It was Friday; and she had fifty cents of her last week's wages.

The streets were filled with the rush-hour floods of people. The electric lights of Broadway were glowing—calling moths from miles, from leagues, from hundreds of leagues out of darkness around to come in and attend the singeing school. Men in accurate clothes, with faces like those carved on cherry-stones by the old salts in sailors' homes, turned and stared at Dulcie as she sped, unheeding, past them. Manhattan, the night-blooming cereus, was beginning to unfold its dead-white, heavy-odored petals.

Dulcie stopped in a store where goods were cheap and bought an imitation lace collar with her fifty cents. That money was to have been spent otherwise—fifteen cents for supper, ten cents for breakfast, ten cents for lunch. Another dime was to be added to her small store of savings; and five cents was to be squandered for liquorice drops—the kind that made your cheek look like the tooth-ache, and last as long. The liquorice was an extravagance—almost a carouse—but what is life without pleasures?

Dulcie lived in a furnished room. There is this difference between a furnished room and a boarding-house. In a furnished room, other people do not know it when you go hungry.

Dulcie went up to her room—the third-floor-back in a West Side brownstone-front. She lit the gas. Scientists tell us that the diamond is the hardest substance known. Their mistake. Landladies know of a compound beside which the diamond is as putty. They pack it in the tips of gas-burners;† and one may stand on a chair and dig at it in vain until one's fingers are pink and bruised. A hairpin will not remove it; therefore let us call it immovable.

So Dulcie lit the gas. In its one-fourth-candle-power† glow we will observe the room.

Couch-bed, dresser, table, washstand, chair—of this much the landlady was guilty. The rest was Dulcie's. On the dresser were her treasures—a gilt china vase presented to her by Sadie, a calendar issued by a pickle works, a book on the divination of dreams, some rice powder in a glass dish, and a cluster of artificial cherries tied with a pink ribbon.

Against the wrinkly mirror stood pictures of General Kitchener,† William Muldoon,† the Duchess of Marlborough,† and Benvenuto Cellini.† Against one wall was a plaster of Paris plaque of an O'Callahan in a Roman helmet. Near it was a violent oleograph of a lemon-colored child assaulting an inflammatory butterfly. This was Dulcie's final judgment in art; but it had never been upset. Her rest had never been disturbed by whispers of stolen copes; no critic had elevated his eyebrows at her infantile entomologist.

Piggy was to call for her at seven. While she swiftly makes ready, let us discreetly face the other way and gossip.

For the room, Dulcie paid two dollars per week. On weekdays her breakfast cost ten cents; she made coffee and cooked an egg over the gaslight while she was dressing. On Sunday mornings she feasted royally on veal chops and pineapple fritters at "Billy's" restaurant, at a cost of twenty-five cents—and tipped the waitress ten cents. New York presents so many temptations for one to run into extravagance. She had her lunches in the department-store restaurant at a cost of sixty cents for the week; dinners were $1.05. The evening papers—show me a New Yorker going without his daily paper!—came to six cents; and two Sunday papers—one for the personal column and the other to read—were ten cents. The total amounts to $4.76. Now, one has to buy clothes, and—

I give it up. I hear of wonderful bargains in fabrics, and of miracles performed with needle and thread; but I am in doubt. I hold my pen poised in vain when I would add to Dulcie's life some of those joys that belong to woman by virtue of all the unwritten, sacred, natural, inactive ordinances of the equity of heaven. Twice she had been to Coney Island and had ridden the hobby-horses. 'Tis a weary thing to count your pleasures by summers instead of by hours.

Piggy needs but a word. When the girls named him, an undeserving stigma was cast upon the noble family of swine. The words-of-three-letters lesson in the old blue spelling-book begins with Piggy's biography. He was fat; he had the soul of a rat, the habits of a bat, and the magnanimity of a cat. He wore expensive clothes; and was a connoisseur in starvation. He could look at a shop-girl and tell you to an hour how long it had been since she had eaten anything more nourishing than marshmallows and tea. He hung about the shopping districts, and prowled around in department stores with his invitations to dinner. Men who escort dogs upon the streets at the end of a string look down upon him. He is a type; I can dwell upon him no longer; my pen is not the kind intended for him; I am no carpenter.

At ten minutes to seven Dulcie was ready. She looked at herself in the wrinkly mirror. The reflection was satisfactory. The dark blue dress, fitting without a wrinkle, the hat with its jaunty black feather, the but-slightly-soiled gloves—all representing self-denial, even of food itself—were vastly becoming.

Dulcie forgot everything else for a moment except that she was beautiful, and that life was about to lift a corner of its mysterious veil for her to observe its wonders. No gentleman had ever asked her out before. Now she was going for a brief moment into the glitter and exalted show.

The girls said that Piggy was a "spender." There would be a grand dinner, and music, and splendidly dressed ladies to look at, and things to eat that strangely twisted the girls' jaws when they tried to tell about them. No doubt she would be asked out again.

There was a blue pongee suit in a window that she knew—by saving twenty cents a week instead of ten, in—let's see—Oh, it would run into years! But there was a second-hand store in Seventh Avenue where—

Somebody knocked at the door. Dulcie opened it. The landlady stood there with a spurious smile, sniffing for cooking by stolen gas.

"A gentleman's downstairs to see you," she said. "Name is Mr. Wiggins."

By such epithet was Piggy known to unfortunate ones who had to take him seriously.

Dulcie turned to the dresser to get her handkerchief; then she stopped still, and bit her underlip hard. While looking in her mirror she had seen fairyland and herself, a princess, just awakening from a long slumber. She had forgotten one that was watching her with sad, beautiful, stern eyes—the only one there was to approve or condemn what she did. Straight and slender and tall, with a look of sorrowful reproach on his handsome, melancholy face, General Kitchener fixed his wonderful eyes on her out of his gilt photograph frame on the dresser.

Dulcie turned like an automatic doll to the land-lady.

"Tell him I can't go," she said dully. "Tell him I'm sick, or something. Tell him I'm not going out."

After the door was closed and locked, Dulcie fell upon her bed, crushing her black tip, and cried for ten minutes. General Kitchener was her only friend. He was Dulcie's ideal of a gallant knight. He looked as if he might have a secret sorrow, and his wonderful moustache was a dream, and she was a little afraid of that stern yet tender look in his eyes. She used to have little fancies that he would call at the house some time, and ask for her, with his sword clanking against his high boots. Once, when a boy was rattling a piece of chain against a lamp-post she had opened the window and looked out. But there was no use. She knew that General Kitchener was away over in Japan, leading his army against the savage Turks; and he would never step out of his gilt frame for her. Yet one look from him had vanquished Piggy that night. Yes, for that night.

When her cry was over Dulcie got up and took off her best dress, and put on her old blue kimono. She wanted no dinner. She sang two verses of "Sammy." Then she became intensely interested in a little red speck on the side of her nose. And after that was attended to, she drew up a chair to the rickety table, and told her fortune with an old deck of cards.

"The horrid, impudent thing!" she said aloud. "And I never gave him a word or a look to make him think it!"

At nine o'clock Dulcie took a tin box of crackers and a little pot of raspberry jam out of her trunk, and had a feast. She offered General Kitchener some jam on a cracker; but he only looked at her as the Sphinx[†] would have looked at a butterfly—if there are butterflies in the desert.

"Don't eat if you don't want to," said Dulcie. "And don't put on so many airs and scold so with your eyes. I wonder if you'd be so superior and snippy if you had to live on six dollars a week."

It was not a good sign for Dulcie to be rude to General Kitchener. And then she turned Benvenuto Cellini face downward with a severe gesture. But that was not inexcusable; for she had always thought he was Henry VIII,† and she did not approve of him.

At half-past nine Dulcie took a last look at the pictures on the dresser, turned out the light, and skipped into bed. It's an awful thing to go to bed with a good-night look at General Kitchener, William Muldoon, the Duchess of Marlborough, and Benvenuto Cellini.

This story really doesn't get anywhere at all. The rest of it comes later—some time when Piggy asks Dulcie again to dine with him, and she is feeling lonelier than usual, and General Kitchener happens to be looking the other way; and then—

As I said before, I dreamed that I was standing near a crowd of prosperous-looking angels, and a policeman took me by the wing and asked if I belonged with them.

"Who are they?" I asked.

"Why," said he, "they are the men who hired working-girls, and paid 'em five or six dollars a week to live on. Are you one of the bunch?"

"Not on your immortality," said I. "I'm only the fellow that set fire to an orphan asylum, and murdered a blind man for his pennies."

BABES IN THE JUNGLE

MONTAGUE SILVER, THE finest street man and art grafter in the West, says to me once in Little Rock: "If you ever lose your mind, Billy, and get too old to do honest swindling† among grown men, go to New York. In the West a sucker is born every minute; but in New York they appear in chunks of roe—you can't count 'em!"

Two years afterward I found that I couldn't remember the names of the Russian admirals, and I noticed some gray hairs over my left ear; so I knew the time had arrived for me to take Silver's advice.

I struck New York about noon one day, and took a walk up Broadway. And I run against Silver himself, all encompassed up in a spacious kind of haberdashery, leaning against a hotel and rubbing the half-moons on his nails with a silk handkerchief.

"Paresis or superannuated?" I asks him.

"Hello, Billy," says Silver; "I'm glad to see you. Yes, it seemed to me that the West was accumulating a little too much wiseness. I've been saving New York for dessert. I know it's a low-down trick to take things from these people. They only know this and that and pass to and fro and think ever and anon. I'd hate for my mother to know I was skinning these weak-minded ones. She raised me better."

"Is there a crush already in the waiting rooms of the old doctor that does skin grafting?" I asks.

"Well, no," says Silver; "you needn't back Epidermis to win today. I've only been here a month. But I'm ready to begin; and the members of Willie

Manhattan's Sunday School class, each of whom has volunteered to contribute a portion of cuticle toward this rehabilitation, may as well send their photos to the *Evening Daily*.

"I've been studying the town," says Silver, "and reading the papers every day, and I know it as well as the cat in the City Hall knows an O'Sullivan. People here lie down on the floor and scream and kick when you are the least bit slow about taking money from them. Come up in my room and I'll tell you. We'll work the town together, Billy, for the sake of old times."

Silver takes me up in a hotel. He has a quantity of irrelevant objects lying about.

"There's more ways of getting money from these metropolitan hayseeds," says Silver, "than there is of cooking rice in Charleston, S. C. They'll bite at anything. The brains of most of 'em commute. The wiser they are in intelligence the less perception of cognizance they have. Why, didin't a man the other day sell J. P. Morgan† an oil portrait of Rockefeller, Jr.,† for Andrea del Sarto's† celebrated painting of the young Saint John!

"You see that bundle of printed stuff in the corner, Billy? That's gold mining stock. I started out one day to sell that, but I quit it in two hours. Why? Got arrested for blocking the street. People fought to buy it. I sold the policeman a block of it on the way to the station-house, and then I took it off the market. I don't want people to give me their money. I want some little consideration connected with the transaction to keep my pride from being hurt. I want 'em to guess the missing letter in Chic-go, or draw to a pair of nines before they pay me a cent of money.

"Now there's another little scheme that worked so easy I had to quit it. You see that bottle of blue ink on the table? I tattooed an anchor on the back of my hand and went to a bank and told 'em I was Admiral Dewey's† nephew. They offered to cash my draft on him for a thousand, but I didn't know my uncle's first name. It shows, though, what an easy town it is. As for burglars, they won't go in a house now unless there's a hot supper ready and a few college students to wait on 'em. They're slugging citizens all over the upper part of the city and I guess, taking the town from end to end, it's a plain case of assault and Battery."†

"Monty," says I, when Silver had slacked up, "you may have Manhattan correctly discriminated in your perorative, but I doubt it. I've only been in town two hours, but it don't dawn upon me that it's ours with a cherry in it. There ain't enough rus in urbe† about it to suit me. I'd be a good deal much better satisfied if the citizens had a straw or more in their hair, and run more to velveteen vests and buckeye watch charms. They don't look easy to me."

"You've got it, Billy," says Silver. "All emigrants have it. New York's bigger than Little Rock or Europe, and it frightens a foreigner. You'll be all right. I tell you I feel like slapping the people here because they don't send me all their money in laundry baskets, with germicide sprinkled over it. I hate to go down on the street to get it. Who wears the diamonds in this town? Why, Winnie, the Wiretapper's wife, and Bella, the Buncosteerer's bride. New Yorkers can be worked easier than a blue rose on a tidy. The only thing that bothers me is I know I'll break the cigars in my vest pocket when I get my clothes all full of twenties."

"I hope you are right, Monty," says I; "but I wish all the same I had been satisfied with a small business in Little Rock. The crop of farmers is never so short out there but what you can get a few of 'em to sign a petition for a new post office that you can discount for $200 at the county bank. The people here appear to possess instincts of self-preservation and illiberality. I fear me that we are not cultured enough to tackle this game."

"Don't worry," says Silver. "I've got this Jayville-near-Tarrytown correctly estimated as sure as North River is the Hudson and East River ain't a river. Why, there are people living in four blocks of Broadway who never saw any kind of a building except a skyscraper in their lives! A good, live hustling Western man ought to get conspicuous enough here inside of three months to incur either Jerome's clemency or Lawson's displeasure."

"Hyperbole aside," says I, "do you know of any immediate system of buncoing the community out of a dollar or two except by applying to the Salvation Army or having a fit on Miss Helen Gould's[†] doorsteps?"

"Dozens of 'em," says Silver. "How much capital have you got, Billy?"

"A thousand," I told him.

"I've got $1,200," says he. "We'll pool and do a big piece of business. There's so many ways we can make a million that I don't know how to begin."

The next morning Silver meets me at the hotel and he is all sonorous and stirred with a kind of silent joy.

"We're to meet J. P. Morgan this afternoon," says he. "A man I know in the hotel wants to introduce us. He's a friend of his. He says he likes to meet people from the West."

"That sounds nice and plausible," says I. "I'd like to know Mr. Morgan."

"It won't hurt us a bit," says Silver, "to get acquainted with a few finance kings. I kind of like the social way New York has with strangers."

The man Silver knew was named Klein. At three o'clock Klein brought his Wall Street friend to see us in Silver's room. "Mr. Morgan" looked some like his pictures, and he had a Turkish towel wrapped around his left foot, and he walked with a cane.

"Mr. Silver and Mr. Pescud," says Klein. "It sounds superfluous," says he, "to mention the name of the greatest financial—"

"Cut it out, Klein," says Mr. Morgan. "I'm glad to know you gents; I take great interest in the West. Klein tells me you're from Little Rock. I think I've a railroad or two out there somewhere. If either of you guys would like to deal a hand or two of stud poker I—"

"Now, Pierpont," cuts in Klein, "you forget!"

"Excuse me, gents!" says Morgan; "since I've had the gout so bad I sometimes play a social game of cards at my house. Neither of you never knew One-eyed Peters, did you, while you was around Little Rock? He lived in Seattle, New Mexico."

Before we could answer, Mr. Morgan hammers on the floor with his can and begins to walk up and down, swearing in a loud tone of voice.

"They have been pounding your stocks to-day on the Street, Pierpont?" asks Klein, smiling.

"Stocks! No!" roars Mr. Morgan. "It's that picture I sent an agent to Europe to buy. I just thought about it. He cabled me to-day that it ain't to be found in all Italy. I'd pay $50,000 tomorrow for that picture—yes, $75,000. I give the agent a la carte in purchasing it. I cannot understand why the art galleries will allow a De Vinchy† to—"

"Why, Mr. Morgan," says Klein; "I thought you owned all of the De Vinchy paintings."

"What is the picture like, Mr. Morgan?" asks Silver. "It must be as big as the side of the Flatiron Building."†

"I'm afraid your art education is on the bum, Mr. Silver," says Morgan. "The picture is 27 inches by 42; and it is called 'Love's Idle Hour.' It represents a number of cloak models doing the two-step on the bank of a purple river. The cablegram said it might have been brought to this country. My collection will never be complete without that picture. Well, so long, gents; us financiers must keep early hours."

Mr. Morgan and Klein went away together in a cab. Me and Silver talked about how simple and unsuspecting great people was; and Silver said what a shame it would be to try to rob a man like Mr. Morgan; and I said I thought it would be rather imprudent, myself. Klein proposes a stroll after dinner; and me and him and Silver walks down toward Seventh Avenue to see the sights. Klein sees a pair of cuff links that instigate his admiration in a pawnshop window, and we all go in while he buys 'em.

After we got back to the hotel and Klein had gone, Silver jumps at me and waves his hands.

"Did you see it?" says he. "Did you see it, Billy?"

"What?" I asks.

"Why, that picture that Morgan wants. It's hanging in that pawnshop, behind the desk. I didn't say anything because Klein was there. It's the article sure as you live. The girls are as natural as paint can make them, all measuring 36 and 25 and 42 skirts, if they had any skirts, and they're doing a buck-and-wing on the bank of a river with the blues. What did Mr. Morgan say he'd give for it? Oh, don't make me tell you. They can't know what it is in that pawnshop."

When the pawnshop opened the next morning me and Silver was standing there as anxious as if we wanted to soak our Sunday suit to buy a drink. We sauntered inside, and began to look at watch-chains.

"That's a violent specimen of a chromo you've got up there," remarked Silver, casual, to the pawnbroker. "But I kind of enthuse over the girl with the shoulderblades and red bunting. Would an offer of $2.25 for it cause you to knock over any fragile articles of your stock in hurrying it off the nail?"

The pawnbroker smiles and goes on showing us plate watch-chains.

"That picture," says he, "was pledged a year ago by an Italian gentleman. I loaned him $500 on it. It is called 'Love's Idle Hour,' and it is by Leonardo de Vinchy. Two days ago the legal time expired, and it became an unredeemed pledge. Here is a style of chain that is worn a great deal now."

At the end of half an hour me and Silver paid the pawnbroker $2,000 and walked out with the picture. Silver got into a cab with it and started for Morgan's office. I goes to the hotel and waits for him. In two hours Silver comes back.

"Did you see Mr. Morgan?" I asks. "How much did he pay you for it?"

Silver sits down and fools with a tassel on the table cover.

"I never exactly saw Mr. Morgan," he says, "because Mr. Morgan's been in Europe for a month. But what's worrying me, Billy, is this: The department stores have all got that same picture on sale, framed, for $3.48. And they charge $3.50 for the frame alone—that's what I can't understand."

The Call of the Tame

WHEN THE INAUGURATION was accomplished—the proceedings were made smooth by the presence of the Rough Riders†—it is well known that a herd of those competent and loyal ex-warrriors paid a visit to the big city. The newspaper reporters dug out of their trunks the old broad-brimmed hats and leather belts that they wear to North Beach fish fries, and mixed with the visitors. No damage was done beyond the employment of the wonderful plural "tenderfeet" in each of the scribe's stories. The Westerners mildly contemplated the skyscrapers as high as the third story, yawned at Broadway, hunched down in the big chairs in hotel corridors, and altogether looked as bored and dejected as a member of Ye Ancient and Honorable Artillery separated during a sham battle from his valet.

Out of this sightseeing delegation of good King Teddy's Gentlemen of the Royal Bear-hounds† dropped one Greenbrier Nye, of Pin Feather, Ariz.

The daily cyclone of Sixth Avenue's rush hour swept him away from the company of his pardners true. The dust from a thousand rustling skirts filled his eyes. The mighty roar of trains rushing across the sky deafened him. The lightning-flash of twice ten hundred beaming eyes confused his vision.

The storm was so sudden and tremendous that Greenbrier's first impulse was to lie down and grab a root. And then he remembered that the disturbance was human, and not elemental; and he backed out of it with a grin into a doorway.

The reporters had written that but for the wide brimmed hats the West was not visible upon these gauchos of the North. Heaven sharpen their eyes! The suit of black diagonal, wrinkled in impossible places; the bright blue four-in-hand, factory tied; the low, turned-down collar, pattern of the days of Seymour and Blair,† white glazed as the letters on the window of the open-day-and-night-except-Sunday restaurants; the out-curve at the knees from the saddle grip; the peculiar spread of the half-closed right thumb and fingers from the stiff hold upon the circling lasso; the deeply absorbed weather tan that the hottest sun of Cape May can never equal; the seldom-winking blue eyes that unconsciously divided the rushing crowds into fours, as though they were being counted out of a corral; the segregated loneliness and solemnity of expression, as of an Emperor or of one whose horizons have not intruded upon him nearer than a day's ride—these brands of the West were set upon Greenbrier Nye. Oh, yes; he wore a broad-brimmed hat, gentle reader—just like those the Madison Square Post Office mail carriers wear when they go up to Bronx Park on Sunday afternoons.

Suddenly Greenbrier Nye jumped into the drifting herd of metropolitan cattle, seized upon a man, dragged him out of the stream and gave him a buffet upon his collarbone that sent him reeling against a wall.

The victim recovered his hat, with the angry look of a New Yorker who has suffered an outrage and intends to write to the Trib. about it. But he looked at his assailant, and knew that the blow was in consideration of love and affection after the manner of the West, which greets its friends with contumely and uproar and pounding fists, and receives its enemies in decorum and order, such as the judicious placing of the welcoming bullet demands.

"God in the mountains!" cried Greenbrier, holding fast to the foreleg of his cull. "Can this be Longhorn Merritt?"

The other man was—oh, look on Broadway any day for the pattern—business man—latest rolled-brim derby—good barber, business, digestion and tailor.

"Greenbrier Nye!" he exclaimed, grasping the hand that had smitten him. "My dear fellow! So glad to see you! How did you come to—oh, to be sure—the inaugural ceremonies—I remember you joined the Rough Riders. You must come and have luncheon with me, of course."

Greenbrier pinned him sadly but firmly to the wall with a hand the size, shape and color of a McClellan saddle.

"Longy," he said, in a melancholy voice that disturbed traffic, "what have they been doing to you? You act just like a citizen. They done made you into an inmate of the city directory. You never made no such Johnny Branch execration of yourself as that out on the Gila.† Come and have lunching with me!' You never defined grub by any such terms of reproach in them days."

"I've been living in New York seven years," said Merritt. "It's been eight since we punched cows together in Old Man Garcia's outfit. Well, let's go to a cafe, anyhow. It sounds good to hear it called 'grub' again."

They picked their way through the crowd to a hotel, and drifted, as by a natural law, to the bar.

"Speak up," invited Greenbrier.

"A dry Martini," said Merritt.

"Oh, Lord!" cried Greenbrier; "and yet me and you once saw the same pink Gila monsters crawling up the walls of the same hotel in Canon Diablo! A dry—but let that pass. Whiskey straight—and they're on you."

Merritt smiled, and paid.

They lunched in a small extension of the dining room that connected with the cafe. Merritt dexterously diverted his friend's choice, that hovered over ham and eggs, to a purée of celery, a salmon cutlet, a partridge pie and a desirable salad.

"On the day," said Greenbrier, grieved and thunderous, "when I can't hold but one drink before eating when I meet a friend I ain't seen in eight years at a 2 by 4 table in a thirty-cent town at 1 o'clock on the third day of the week, I want nine broncos to kick me forty times over a 640-acre section of land. Get them statistics?"

"Right, old man," laughed Merritt. "Waiter, bring an absinthe frappe and—what's yours, Greenbrier?"

"Whiskey straight," mourned Nye. "Out of the neck of a bottle you used to take it, Longy—straight out of the neck of a bottle on a galloping pony—Arizona redeye, not this ab—oh, what's the use? They're on you."

Merritt slipped the wine card under his glass.

"All right. I suppose you think I'm spoiled by the city. I'm as good a Westerner as you are, Greenbrier; but, somehow, I can't make up my mind to go back out there. New York is comfortable—comfortable. I make a good living, and I live it. No more wet blankets and riding herd in snowstorms, and bacon and cold coffee, and blowouts once in six months for me. I reckon I'll hang out here in the future. We'll take in the theatre tonight, Greenbrier, and after that we'll dine at—"

"I'll tell you what you are, Merritt," said Greenbrier, laying one elbow in his salad and the other in his butter. "You are a concentrated, effete, unconditional, short-sleeved, gotch-eared Miss Sally Walker. God made you perpendicular and suitable to ride straddle and use cuss words in the original. Wherefore you have suffered his handiwork to elapse by removing yourself to New York and putting on little shoes tied with strings, and making faces when you talk. I've seen you rope and tie a steer in 42 1/2. If you was to see one now you'd write to the Police Commissioner about it. And these flapdoodle drinks that you inoculate your system with—these little essences of cowslip with acorns in 'em, and paregoric flip—they ain't anyways in assent with the cordiality of manhood. I hate to see you this way."

"Well, Mr. Greenbrier," said Merritt, with apology in his tone, "in a way you are right. Sometimes I do feel like I was being raised on the bottle. But, I tell you, New York is comfortable—comfortable. There's something about it—the sights and the crowds, and the way it changes every day, and the very air of it that seems to tie a one-mile-long stake rope around a man's neck, with the other end fastened somewhere about Thirty-fourth Street. I don't know what it is."

"God knows," said Greenbrier sadly, "and I know. The East has gobbled you up. You was venison, and now you're veal. You put me in mind of a japonica in a window. You've been signed, sealed and diskivered. Requiescat in hoc signo.† You make me thirsty."

"A green chartreuse here," said Merritt to the waiter.

"Whiskey straight," sighed Greenbrier, "and they're on you, you renegade of the round-ups."

"Guilty, with an application for mercy," said Merritt. "You don't know how it is, Greenbrier. It's so comfortable here that—"

"Please loan me your smelling salts," pleaded Greenbrier. "If I hadn't seen you once bluff three bluffers from Mazatzal City with an empty gun in Phoenix—"

Greenbrier's voice died away in pure grief.

"Cigars!" he called harshly to the waiter, to hide his emotion.

"A pack of Turkish cigarettes for mine," said Merritt.

"They're on you," chanted Greenbrier, struggling to conceal his contempt.

At seven they dined in the Where-to-Dine-Well column.

That evening a galaxy had assembled there. Bright shone the lights o'er fair women and br—Let it go, anyhow—brave men. The orchestra played charmingly. Hardly had a tip from a diner been placed in its hands by a waiter when it would burst forth into soniferousness. The more beer you contributed to it the more Meyerbeer† it gave you. Which is reciprocity.

Merritt put forth exertions on the dinner. Greenbrier was his old friend, and he liked him. He persuaded him to drink a cocktail.

"I take the horehound tea," said Greenbrier, "for old times' sake. But I'd prefer whiskey straight. They're on you."

"Right!" said Merritt. "Now, run your eye down that bill of fare and see if it seems to hitch on any of these items."

"Lay me on my lava bed!" said Greenbrier, with bulging eyes. "All these specimens of nutriment in the grub wagon! What's this? Horse with the heaves? I pass. But look along! Here's truck for twenty roundups all spelled out in different directions. Wait till I see."

The viands ordered, Merritt turned to the wine list.

"This Medoc isn't bad," he suggested.

"You're the doc," said Greenbrier. "I'd rather have whiskey straight. It's on you."

Greenbrier looked around the room. The waiter brought things and took dishes away. He was observing. He saw a New York restaurant crowd enjoying itself.

"How was the range when you left the Gila?" asked Merritt.

"Fine," said Greenbrier. "You see that lady in the red speckled silk at that table? Well, she could warm over her beans at my campfire. Yes, the range was good. She looks as nice as a white mustang I see once on Black River."

When the coffee came, Greenbrier put one foot on the seat of the chair next to him.

"You said it was a comfortable town, Longy," he said, meditatively. "Yes, it's a comfortable town. It's different from the plains in a blue norther. What did you call that mess in the crock with the handle, Longy? Oh, yes, squabs in a cash roll. They're worth the roll. That white mustang had just such a way of turning his head and shaking his mane—look at her, Longy. If I thought I could sell out my ranch at a fair price, I believe I'd—

"Gyar-song!"† he suddenly cried, in a voice that paralyzed every knife and fork in the restaurant.

The waiter dived toward the table.

"Two more of them cocktail drinks," ordered Greenbrier.

Merritt looked at him and smiled significantly.

"They're on me," said Greenbrier, blowing a puff of smoke to the ceiling.

Glossary

THE FURNISHED ROOM

the lower West Side – a section of Manhattan, a borough of New York City; New York City is the setting for a large number of O. Henry's stories. The book in which this story was originally published is titled *The Four Million,* which refers to the large number of people living in New York during O. Henry's time and the fact that each one has an individual story to tell. By the 2000 Census, though, New York City's population had grown to slightly more than eight million.

"Home, Sweet Home" – a song from the American opera *Clari, the Maid of Milan*, written by John Howard Payne in 1823

ragtime – a style of jazz music popular from the 1890s through the 1920s

"lares et penates" – [*Latin*] loosely translated as "household gods and guardians"; the phrase is commonly meant to refer to highly valued household possessions.

picture hat – a decorative wide-brimmed hat for women

"unwholesome, surfeited worm" – The narrator likens the landlady to a worm, commonly thought to be one of the lowliest creatures on Earth. Watch for more references to worms throughout the story, along with references to fungus and dank, underground things. The greedy and amoral landlady is represented by these descriptions.

"its own loom would have forsworn" – an example of personification; O. Henry is representing the carpet and its loom as if they are people, instead of unthinking, inanimate objects that they really are. The implication in the comparison is that the loom that made the carpet would have denied that it had actually done so because of the worn quality of the carpet. Note that later in the story, the entire room and its furnishings are personified as well (see note: *Mr. Pneumonia* in *The Last Leaf* glossary).

water-girt – literally, *surrounded by water*; the island of Manhattan is bound by the East River and the Hudson River.

"demirep" – [*slang*] a promiscuous woman; the term literally means "half a reprobate." *Reprobate* refers to a person of loose morals or one who is evil and beyond redemption.

"confused in speech...apartment in Babel" – a reference to Babel, a city mentioned in the Old Testament. According to the Bible, Noah's descendants attempted to build a giant tower reaching to heaven because they believed their unified culture could accomplish anything, and that the tower would be a source of pride and admiration for them. God, however, did not want the people to exhibit such pride because it showed that they were glorifying themselves instead of God; therefore, He confused the people's language and scattered them across the earth.

Huguenot – a French Protestant living during the sixteenth and seventeenth centuries

Psyche at the Fountain – part of the Greek myth of Cupid and Psyche; Psyche was a woman who fell in love with and married the god, Cupid, and became immortal.

"**...the couch...seemed a horrible monster.**" – an example of an implied simile; O. Henry compares the couch to a monster, but without using *like* or *as*.

"**rayjict**" – [*dialect*] the word *reject*, spoken in Mrs. McCool's Irish accent

a colleen – an Irish girl

"**...but for that mole she...left eyebrow.**" – Here, readers learn that the dead young girl the women are talking about is, in fact, the young girl that the protagonist has been seeking. This type of surprise twist ending is a trademark of many of O. Henry's short stories.

THE LAST LEAF

Greenwich Village – a neighborhood in lower Manhattan noted for its community of artists, writers, and musicians

"***table d'hôte***" – [*French*] translated as "host's table"; a group table in a restaurant at which any of the diners can sit

"**Delmonico's**" – a chain of family-owned restaurants in New York City operating from 1827 through 1923

bishop sleeves – puffy shirt sleeves that became popular in the mid-to-late nineteenth century

"**Mr. Pneumonia**" – an example of personification

Bay of Naples – a bay in the Mediterranean, near the southwestern coast of Italy

a jew's-harp – a small musical instrument held at the mouth that creates a soft twang when played

"**Michael Angelo's Moses**" – [*Michelangelo*] This is a reference to the famous sculpture by Italian Renaissance artist Michelangelo (1475-1564). In the sculpture, Moses has a long flowing beard that curls down to his lap. The narrator likens Mr. Behrman's appearance to that of Moses.

"**his Mistress's robe**"–The mistress the narrator refers to is Art.

juniper berries – berries from which gin is made

"**Vass!**" – [*German*] "What!" Note that many of O. Henry's stories (especially those set in New York) depict immigrant characters who speak in broken English and with heavy accents. O. Henry's keen ear for dialect is one of the things that make his characters so realistic.

"**Gott!**" – [*German*] "God!"

THE GIFT OF THE MAGI

"One dollar…in pennies." – Note that it is impossible for this amount to be correct mathematically. Della cannot have $1.87 with only $.60 in pennies. No one has offered any credible explanation as to why O. Henry wrote it this way.

"sobs, sniffles, and smiles" – an example of alliteration

"$8 per week" – This would have been the rental cost of an apartment in which a lower middle class New York City couple might live.

Queen of Sheba; King Solomon – In the Old Testament, the wealthy Queen of Sheba, who ruled an ancient kingdom in the region of modern-day Ethiopia, visited the equally wealthy King Solomon of Israel in order to test his wisdom. When the King answered her questions, she was so impressed with his wisdom that she showered him with gold and jewels. He, in turn, granted her everything she desired.

Coney Island – an amusement park and beach resort in Brooklyn, New York; still in operation today, Coney Island was very popular during the early part of the twentieth century, especially among the middle class.

"The magi brought valuable gifts…" – The magi (the "Three Wise Men" in the Bible) paid homage to the baby Jesus by bringing gifts of gold, frankincense, and myrrh.

"…let it be said…were the wisest." – This statement reveals the theme of the story, which relates to the importance of unselfish love having no boundaries. The gifts that James and Della give to one another end up having no useful function or material value, but they are, in fact, the most valuable gifts for either of them to have given. This is evident because they are given purely through love for another person and self-sacrifice.

THE COP AND THE ANTHEM

Vesuvian Bay – the bay off the coast of Naples, Italy; Mount Vesuvius, the volcano, is just six miles from the coast.

"Boreas and bluecoats" – In Greek mythology, Boreas was the god of the northern wind. "Bluecoat" is slang for police officer, due to the blue uniforms the police wore.

Palm Beach – a city in Florida that the wealthy vacationed to during the winter

Riviera – a coastal resort region ranging from southeastern France to northwestern Italy

Sabbath – Sunday, the Christian day of rest

"Caesar had his Brutus" – Julius Caesar ruled the Roman Empire from 46 BC to 44 BC. He was assassinated by Brutus, who had been one of his followers. O. Henry is commenting that every reward comes with a penalty; Soapy might get a bed in which he could sleep, but he would have to bathe.

"…the choicest products…the protoplasm." – Apparently this phrase is referring to wine, silk, and upper-class people. Note the sarcastic tone implied by the word *protoplasm* in contrast with the other two, *grape* and *silkworm*.

four-in-hand – a particular type of necktie

"masher" – [*slang*] a man who makes advances toward women in an unwanted way

"…if you'll blow me to a pail of suds." – The woman means "if you'll buy me a beer."

"He seemed doomed to liberty." – This is an example of verbal irony. The statement contains an incongruous or unexpected point. We do not normally think of liberty (freedom) as something one is "doomed" to. In fact, to be doomed to something is the opposite of having liberty.

Arcadia – a mythological place of tranquility and simplicity

" 'Three months on the Island,' said the Magistrate…" – an example of situational irony; throughout the entire story, Soapy has been trying in vain to get himself arrested so that he can spend the winter in the warmth of the jail. Just when Soapy has decided to stop his vagrant ways and stay out of jail, he is arrested and sent to jail. (The "Island" is Ryker's Island, a jail located in the East River in New York City.) Once again, O. Henry has surprised the reader with an unexpected ending.

THE GREEN DOOR

vaudeville – a type of live entertainment popular in the early twentieth century, consisting of a variety of acts, such as comedy, skits, and song-and-dance routines

Russian sables – extremely expensive furs

"golden fleeces, holy grails" – These are references to much sought-after objects. In Greek mythology, the Golden Fleece was the wool of a golden ram. The Holy Grail is the legendary cup that Jesus is said to have used at the Last Supper.

Prodigal Son – a figure from the New Testament who sinfully wastes his inheritance money, returns to his family, and is forgiven

"From the Crusades to the Palisades…" – The Crusades were a series of wars waged by Christians during the eleventh through the thirteenth centuries against non-Christians in order to reclaim the Holy Land. The Palisades are a section of steep cliffs along the Hudson River in northeastern New Jersey.

Sidereal System – relating to the stars and their constellations

" 'Junie's love Test' by Miss Libbey" – most likely a reference to the romance novels of early twentieth century American writer, Laura Jean Libbey

"Himmel!" – [*German*] heaven, as in the exclamation, "Heaven's, no!"

the Iliad – the epic poem from the eighth century BC by the Greek poet Homer that tells of the Trojan War

After Twenty Years

"Bully" – [*slang*] "great" or "excellent"

A Retrieved Reformation

"stir" – [*slang*] prison

"...the phoenix...Valentine's ashes..." – In ancient Egyptian mythology, the phoenix was a bird, which burned itself every five hundred years and then arose anew from its own ashes. The phoenix is commonly used as a symbol for resurrection or rebirth.

The Third Ingredient

"space-rate writers" – writers, especially reporters or magazine contributors, who are paid by the inch or by the page

Lady Godiva – a noblewoman in the mid-eleventh century Coventry; she protested her husband's heavy tax policy by riding naked through the town on a horse. Her husband Leofric, the Earl of Mercia, supposedly agreed to lighten the tax burden due to her daring ride.

Hercules – a hero from ancient Greek mythology known for his strength and courage

Joan of Arc – a young woman in fifteenth-century France who believed she heard voices from God telling her to fight with the French Resistance against the English during the 100 Years War. She headed several military campaigns and was later burned at the stake for heresy. The Catholic Church canonized her, and she became a saint in 1920.

Una – This may be a reference to a character from *The Faerie Queene*, Edmund Spenser's epic poem that was written in 1590. In the poem, Una persuades a knight to save her family from a dragon.

Job – a man, from the Old Testament, who remained steadfast in his faith in God even as he endured many terrible ordeals; Job is symbolic of faith and patience.

Jolly Roger – the flag traditionally flown by pirate ships, consisting of a skull and cross bones design

Dago – a derogatory ethnic term for a person of Italian descent

"skeeziks" – [*slang*] rascal; here it is probably simply a term of derision.

accelerando – [*Italian*] accelerating in tempo

<u>The Princess and the Puma</u>

The Princess and the Puma – The title may have been a reference to a famous short story by Frank Stockton, entitled "The Lady or the Tiger," written in 1882.

Laredo – a city in southern Texas situated on the Rio Grande near the Mexican border

Colorado-claro – a type of cigar wrapper that is light brown in color; the narrator is referring to the skin color of Ben's Mexican wife.

Danaë – In Greek mythology, Danaë was imprisoned in a bronze tower by her father, the king of Argos. This was because the king was told by an oracle that Danaë would bear a child and that this child would end up killing him. Danaë eventually gave birth to Perseus and the prophecy was fulfilled. It seems that the narrator of the story is alluding to Danaë's imprisonment and not to the rest of the myth.

lese-majesté – [*French*] a crime committed against a ruling power

Nueces country – an area surrounding the Nueces River in southern Texas

Mexican lion – another term for a mountain lion, usually called a puma in southwestern regions of the United States and in Mexico

Momus – in Greek mythology, the god of mockery and ridicule

Cupid – the Roman name for Eros, the Greek god of love

S.P.C.A. – the Society for the Prevention of Cruelty to Animals

<u>Buried Treasure</u>

bucket-shops – fraudulent brokerage firms that swindle investors out of their money

King Midas – a figure from ancient Greek mythology who was granted the power to turn everything he touched into gold

"**for to have and to hold**" – a phrase used during marriage vows, indicating that the narrator wants to marry the woman he sees

"**He was an etymologist, or words to that effect.**" – This is a pun or malapropism regarding the words *etymologist* and *entomologist*. The narrator means to say *entomologist*, which is a person who studies bugs, but instead, he uses the word *etymologist*, which means one who studies words.

racibus humanus – This is another example of the narrator's misuse of words. He is trying to sound like an intellectual by sprinkling some Latin into his speech, but he gets it wrong. He seems to think that *racibus humanus* would mean "human race" in Latin. While *humanus* does mean man or humankind, *racibus* has no Latin meaning at all.

Orgetorix, Rex Halvetii – another humorous attempt by the narrator to make it appear as if he speaks Latin. Orgetorix was the leader of the Helvetii, a group of people who lived in the area of Switzerland in the first century BC.

charco – [*Spanish*] "puddle"

"a dried, Smyrna, dago-stand fig"– an insulting term indicating worthlessness

"...the rebellion...against the secessionists." – During the American Civil War (1861-1865) the Union, comprised of the northern states and in favor of the abolition of slavery, fought with the southern states, who had seceded from the Union and formed the Confederacy. The joke in this particular phrase is that the narrator speaks of the Union as the part of the country that rebelled, when, in fact, it was the southern states that left the Union.

Fort Worth – a city in northeastern Texas

King Philip of Spain – a reference to King Philip II of Spain (1527-1598), who granted land to colonists in Texas and New Mexico in the sixteenth century

"the roan and the dun" – colors of horses; a roan-colored horse is reddish-brown with white or gray speckles, and a dun-colored horse is grayish-brown.

true meridian – This is an imaginary line on the earth's surface extending from the North Pole to the South Pole and passing through Greenwich, England. Longitude is measured from the prime, or true, meridian, which is at zero degrees.

Anacreon – a Greek poet living around 500 BC, who wrote of wine and love

"Keats...and Kelly or Shelley" – John Keats (1795-1821) and Percy Bysshe Shelley (1792-1822) were two of the greatest English Romantic poets of the nineteenth century, but, once again, the narrator is not sure of the names.

Ulysses – the Roman name for Odysseus, the ancient Greek hero in Homer's epic poem, the *Odyssey*. *Ulysses* is also the title of the great twentieth century novel by James Joyce.

An Unfinished Story

Tophet – according to the Bible, a place near Jerusalem where children were burned alive in sacrifice to the god Moloch; in this story, Tophet is synonymous with hell.

Morpheus – the ancient Roman god of dreams

"Gabriel had played his trump..." – In the Bible, Gabriel, often depicted with a trumpet, was an angel and messenger of God. O. Henry makes this pun, relating to *trump*, a term involved in playing cards, and *trumpet*.

Hamburg edging – a type of machine-embroidered trim for cloth

"They pack it in the tips of gas-burners…" – apparently a practice used by apartment owners to restrict the amount of gas being used by tenants, resulting in a lower gas bill for the "landladies"

one-fourth-candle-power – One candlepower equals the amount of light emitted from one candle, so one-fourth candlepower would be one-fourth the light emitted from one candle; a very small amount.

General Kitchener – apparently Horatio Herbert Kitchener (1850-1916), a British field marshal most famous for his victories in the Second Boer War, which was fought in South Africa from 1899-1902

William Muldoon – (1852-1933) an American wrestling champion and boxing promoter

the Duchess of Marlborough – (1660-1744) Born Sarah Jennings, she was the wife of John Churchill (the Duke of Marlborough) and a close friend to England's Queen Anne.

Benvenuto Cellini – (1500-1571) an Italian sculptor and writer during the Renaissance

Sphinx – a creature from Ancient Egyptian mythology having the body of a lion and the head of a woman

Henry VIII – King of England from 1509 to 1547

Babes In The Jungle

"honest swindling" – an example of an oxymoron, a figure of speech in which words contradict one another; here the narrator seems to be saying that there is honor among thieves and that taking advantage of "grown men" is allowable, especially in New York.

J.P. Morgan – John Pierpont Morgan (1837-1913), a powerful American banker, who was famous for his enterprises in the steel and railroad business, as well as in banking

Rockefeller, Jr. – the son of John D. Rockefeller (1839-1937), who was a famous American industrialist and oil tycoon

Andrea del Sarto – (1486-1531) a Florentine painter during the Italian Renaissance

Admiral Dewey – (1837-1917) American admiral famous for his victories during the Spanish-American War

"assault and Battery" – a pun regarding the word *battery*; the Battery is a park at the southernmost end of Manhattan in New York City.

"rus in urbe"– loosely translated from Latin; basically it means a home near an urban area, but one also having the advantages of the country.

Miss Helen Gould – an early twentieth century American philanthropist famous for her generosity to New York colleges and libraries, among other charities

"De Vinchy" – meaning Leonardo da Vinci (1452-1519), the Italian Renaissance painter, scientist, and engineer, most famous for painting the *Mona Lisa* and *The Last Supper*

Flatiron Building – a New York City building designed by Daniel Burnham in 1902. The building is shaped like a flattened triangle, resembling an iron.

THE CALL OF THE TAME

Rough Riders – members of a cavalry unit led by Theodore Roosevelt during the Spanish-American War

"King Teddy's Gentlemen of the Royal Bear-hounds" – another reference to Roosevelt and his companions

Seymour and Blair – Horatio Seymour and Francis P. Blair, Democratic nominees for president and vice-president in 1868

"the Gila" – a river running from Western New Mexico to Arizona and the valley area around this river

"Requiescat in hoc signo." – [*Latin*] loosely translated as "rest in this sign"

Meyerbeer – Giacomo Meyerbeer (1791-1864), a famous German opera composer

"Gyar-song!" – "*Garçon!*" the French word for "waiter," shouted in Greenbrier's western accent

Vocabulary

THE FURNISHED ROOM

askew – crooked, slanted
bandbox – a small box used to hold clothes
besought – begged, implored
brocade – a type of heavy fabric
cant – tilt, slant
chastely – purely; modestly
cognizant – aware; informed
commingled – mixed, combined
cryptograph – a message in secret code
demure – modest
discourse – talk
divers – [*diverse*] various, miscellaneous
draying – hauling heavy loads on a type low cart (a *dray*)
effluvium – vapor; by-product, waste
flotsam – debris, remains
forbearance – tolerance, patience
forsworn – renounced, rejected
fugacious – fleeting; elusive
garish – showy, gaudy
gaslight – a gas-burning lamp
heliotrope – a type of plant with purple fragrant flowers
ignoble – vulgar, base
incontinent – lacking self-restraint
inert – motionless
inevitable – unavoidable; certain
ingloriously – shamefully, dishonorably
insolent – rude, brazen
lichen – a type of fungus
loom – a machine used for weaving yarn or thread
mignonette – a type of plant with small, green fragrant flowers
mitigated – made less severe; moderated
peremptorily – urgently; emphatically
perfunctory – routine
peripatetic – constantly walking or moving from place to place
pier glass – a large mirror set between two windows
polychromatic – multi-colored
rakishly – carelessly
ransacking – searching recklessly; pillaging
sophistical – plausible-seeming, but actually false or deceptive

specious – deceptive, misleading; false
surfeited – indulged to excess; satisfied
transients – people who move from place to place; homeless people
trenchant – cutting, forceful
viscid – sticky, glue-like
vivified – animated; made lively
whence – from where

THE LAST LEAF
chivalric – noble, dignified
curative – having the ability to heal
dissolution – disintegration; ruin
flibbertigibbet – a frivolous and silly person
mastiff – a large, heavy dog
monocle – an eyeglass made for only one eye
morbid – gruesome
pharmacopeia – an encyclopedia of drugs and their uses
satyr – a mythological creature with characteristics of both man and goat or horse
serrated – uneven; notched; jagged
smiting – harming or killing by a severe blow
solicitously – with care; concern
zephyrs – gentle winds

THE GIFT OF THE MAGI
appertaining – relating
ardent – eager, passionate
assertion – a statement, claim
coveted – desired, wanted
depreciate – to devalue, cheapen
ecstatic – overjoyed, elated
fob – a chain connected to a pocket watch
imputation – an accusation, charge
instigates – incites; urges on
laboriously – with much effort
longitudinal – in vertical measurements
mendicancy – the condition of being in poverty
meretricious – showy or flashy in a cheap way
parsimony – thriftiness, frugality
predominating – prevalent; having more power
vestibule – an entryway

THE COP AND THE ANTHEM

accordant – in agreement
accusive – characterized by an accusation
anthem – a sacred song of praise
benign – good
brazenly – shamelessly
conjunction – joining; union
contiguity – proximity, nearness
convolutions – intricate twists and turns
decadent – in a state of decay
demeanor – an attitude or behavior
demitasse – a small cup of strong coffee
denizens – inhabitants
disconsolate – sad, dejected
eleemosynary – having to do with charity
encumbered – burdened, impaired
epicurean – related to sensual pleasures
execrated – denounced, hated
faltering – weakening in purpose
fatuously – foolishly
greatcoats – large overcoats
guise – the appearance
hegira – a flight; exodus
hibernatorial – characterized by sleeping through the winter
impudent – unwise; lacking good judgement
insolvency – bankruptcy; poverty
insular – isolated
librettos – the written texts of musical works, especially operas
litany – a long list of complaints
magistrate – a judge
manifestation – a demonstration of power; a ghostlike materialization
minions – servant-like followers
napery – table linen
parley – to discuss with an enemy
philanthropy – charity
presentiment – a premonition; expectation
pretensions – false claims of superiority
protoplasm – cellular matter in living organisms
receptive – open and responsive
sidled – moved along in a sideways manner
soporific – sleepy; tranquil
transfixed – unable to move; riveted

transplendent – brilliantly lit
welkin – the sky
wherefore – why

THE GREEN DOOR

allurement – an enticement, attraction
ardour – passion
babel – a confusion of languages
bereft – deprived; lacking something
beseige – to surround; to crowd
blusteringly – in a loud and noisy way
consummation – a completion; to finish
contingent – a group that has something in common
contumelious – arrogant; scornful
countenance – facial appearance
domesticity – the quality of being involved with household affairs
egregious – outrageous, extreme
eloquently – in an articulate way; fluently
enigma – a puzzle
expedient – a necessity in order to do something quickly
gaudy – showy, flashy
lattices – woven strips
mercenary – motivated by money
millinery – a business of making and selling women's hats
pallid – pale
parallelogram – four-sided shape
polyglot – speaking multiple languages
prodigal – wasteful and careless spending of money
rapturous – elated, overjoyed
temerarious – reckless; rash
tierce – a position in the sport of fencing
wan – pale

AFTER TWENTY YEARS

egotism – self-centeredness
nigh – near
pacific – peaceful, tranquil
stalwart – strong; resolute
staunchest – most devoted; truest

A Retrieved Reformation

alterative – liable to be changed
amalgamated – blended; joined
assiduously – in a hard-working and attentive way; diligently
augers – tools used for making holes
balked – refused
burglarious – pertaining to burglary
clemency – mercy; leniency
compulsory – mandatory, forced
confederates – associates
eminent – distinguished, celebrated
genially – cordially, warmly
gilded – ornamented; attractive in appearance
guile – deceit, dishonesty
implements – equipment, tools
livery – the business of renting out horses and carriages
retribution – revenge; punishment
unobtrusively – in an unnoticed manner, inconspicuously

The Third Ingredient

acetic – pertaining to vinegar
barque – a type of sailing ship
bearded – confronted
boudoir – a private room for a woman
browbeaten – intimidated, bullied
cloying – excessively sweet
commissary – a food and supplies store
delectable – delicious, tasty
dirk – a long dagger
figuratively – in a representational way
frangipanni – type of fragrant shrub
gimlets – small tools used for boring holes
guy – to mock or to ridicule
haughtily – arrogantly, proudly
hove – came into position, lingered; floated; waited
kimonos – Japanese-style robes
levied – imposed a tax
lithography – a type of printing process
lugubrious – exaggerated melancholy or depression
metaphorically – in a symbolic or figurative way
modiste – a maker of or dealer in women's fashions
omnipresent – present everywhere and all the time

omniscient – all-knowing
omnivorous – eating or consuming any type of food
paroxysm – a convulsion, spasm
phalanx – an army, brigade
portal – an entranceway
preordained – decreed or ordered in advance
profusion – an abundance
protracted – prolonged
punctiliously – politely, mannerly
pungent – sharp in taste or smell
sapient – to bewise
sinewy – lean, muscular
temperament – disposition; character
victual – food
waylayer – someone who accosts another person

THE PRINCESS AND THE PUMA
aggrieved – hurt, injured
arroyos – deep gullies with water running through them
contralto – a low female voice
demurred – objected
fiasco – a failure; blunder
formidable – dreadful, fearful
gar – a type of large pond fish
ignominiously – shamefully, disgracefully
indisputable – undeniable; certain
intrepidity – bravery, courage
magnanimity – generosity; kindness; ability to deal with problems calmy
mesquite – a type of thorny bush
penitently – with sorrow and apology; remorsefully
pensively – in a thoughtful way
presumptuous – arrogant; brash
proffered – offered, presented
reproach – disapproval; condemnation
saccharine – sweet
sacuista – type of grass that grows in clumps
sojourner – a tenant, lodger
tentatively – hesitantly, uncertainly
vassal – a slave, servant
yearlings – animals that are only one year old

BURIED TREASURE

appendage – something attached to another, larger thing
assimilated – incorporated into; absorbed; made similar
attainments – accomplishments, achievements
buckboard – a horse-drawn buggy
cavalcade – a parade, procession
chattels – property, goods
clodhopper – a clumsy or unrefined person
concavity – a depression, cavity, the quality of being concave
cupidity – excessive desire
deflect – to divert, veer
dove-cot – a house for pigeons or doves
draughtsman – someone who sketches designs or plans
etymologist – one who studies words and their origins
forded – crossed a body of water at the shallow point
furor – a frenzy; madness
hypotenuse – move in a right triangle to the end, the side which is opposite the right angle
imprudently – carelessly or recklessly, unwisely
increment – an increase, addition
lorn – forsaken
monopoly – exclusive possession and control
non-arable – unfit for growing or cultivating
oracle – a person who is able to predict the future
palpable – obvious, evident; able to be touched
patrimony – an inheritance
sardonic – sarcastic; bitter
seining – fishing with a large net
solemnity – seriousness
varas – units of measurement, approximately one yard
vertebrates – animals having a spinal column
water-mark – a design imprinted on paper by the manufacturer

AN UNFINISHED STORY

carouse – drunken merry-making
connoisseur – an expert
controverted – disputed; argued against
copes – long capes
divination – interpretation of omens; foretelling
entomologist – one who studies insects
epithet – an abusive name; an insult
equity – justice, fairness

ether – atmosphere, air
exalted – high-ranking; magnificent
inflammatory – arousing strong emotion
irrelevant – unrelated, inapplicable
medulla oblongata – the part of the brain that controls most bodily functions
oleograph – a printed picture made to look like an oil painting
ordinances – laws, rules
orthodoxy – an adherence to traditional beliefs; conformity
pongee – a type of silk cloth
radium – a radioactive element
spurious – false, phony
squandered – spent wastefully
unheeding – thoughtless; oblivious
vanquished – conquered

BABES IN THE JUNGLE

buncoing – swindling
cognizance – awareness; thought
emigrants – displaced people, migrants, a person who leaves their home contry to live in another
gout – a swelling of the leg or joints
grafter – a swindler
haberdashery – men's accessories
hyperbole – exaggeration
illiberality – selfishness, stinginess; not genersous, miserliness
paresis – partial paralysis
perorative – the concluding part of a speech
roe – fish eggs
sonorous – having a deep, rich sound
superannuated – retired; obsolete
superfluous – excessive; unnecessary

THE CALL OF THE TAME

absinthe – a type of alcoholic liqueur
contumely – arrogance, nerve
cull – something gathered or picked out
dexterously – skillfully, expertly
effete – unproductive, worn-out
execration – hatred, loathing
gauchos – South American cowboys
inauguration – a formal ceremony to install a person in office
japonica – a type of flowering shrub
purée – food that is strained into a liquid
reciprocity – give and take; exchange
soniferousness – the condition of producing sound
tenderfeet – inexperienced people; newcomers
viands – food items